Dedication

To Robert C. Brown, boss, mentor, and
friend extraordinaire.

* * *

One

Ellen was awake. Davis could hear her crying softly as he stepped onto the back porch. He was saddened, but not surprised. His wife often cried first thing in the morning. Cancer was a tough load to bear.

He crossed under the grape arbor and climbed the mound of earth that covered the root cellar. Then he looked west, out across the garden and the D.C. Groves place, and then the white curve of road beyond. In this section of Pratt County, the land ran flat and smooth, and on a clear day a man could see all the way to Kansas. For just about all his life, Davis Wells had been thinking about crossing over to Kansas, leaving Missouri and all his problems behind. In the early hour, Kansas still lay draped in the smoky blue shadows of morning.

For a moment, he stared toward Kansas, then turned slowly, looking north first, gazing out over the old family cemetery and the fields where his father had planted wheat and corn, then east, down the slope, past the henhouse to the barn. Beyond the barn was the pasture his father's cows had grazed. His eyes drifted south, following the gravel drive until it reached Highway H, then on across the asphalt up another drive to a ramshackledly wooden house where old Mrs. Monroe had lived.

The first blush of sunlight was warm on his face as he sipped coffee and let his mind drift. First to when he'd been a kid and lived on the farm with his mom and dad, both gone now, and then to crossing over to Kansas. Davis' brain ached as he drank coffee and studied on just what the hell he was supposed to do. Living like a monk wasn't much of a life. Undesired celibacy made him think about things that made his guts churn and kept him awake at night.

"Davis? Davis? You out there?"

He swallowed the coffee in his mouth and tossed the rest across the grass. Ellen was up and she needed him. Every day now she needed him. Being needed wasn't the smoothest road, but he figured he just had to hump up and keep going, at least for now.

~ * ~

Deep in the shadows of a copse of oak and hickories that had been young when the country was settled, a man and woman stood quietly. The man raised a pair of binoculars to his eyes and swept the slope of land to the house, then the house, before settling on the rise of ground covering the root cellar.

"There he is, the son-of-a-bitch who ran me out of my own county."

"Lawton, you know he's the law. He's bound to be trouble."

"I know he's going to find himself with more trouble than he can handle."

"Honey, nobody knows where you are. We can go somewhere and start fresh. With your contacts, you can get us all the I.D. we need for a new life. One where we won't have to be always looking over our shoulder."

The man lowered the binoculars and stared across the morning at another man, a man he planned to make suffer. "After I take care of Davis Wells. After that."

~ * ~

A thin mist still held in the swale on the far side of the garden. A prone figure groaned and a meadowlark whirled into flight. The figure rose onto one elbow and blinked his eyes open. Slowly, the figure sat up, revealing himself to be a man—a short, thin man with a scraggly beard, long greasy hair, and bloodshot eyes. He rubbed at those eyes, pushed his body upright and stood swaying gently with the mist swirling around his face like chilled smoke.

Turning slowly, he surveyed the landscape, trying to get his bearings, some sense of where he was. He struggled to recall the night before, but all he could remember was meeting a scumbag known as Dirty John in an alley behind Lovett's Hardware. Considering the shape he was in, the man in the morning, known to friends and family as Birdman, figured he must have bought some damn fine shit. Only he couldn't remember the buy, the high, or where he'd gotten the jack to fly.

Birdman let his eyes sweep across the open field before him, then the road, before he swung his eyes to the west. A light flashed at him from a grove of trees and he dropped to one knee as he peered through the shimmering mist. It took him a couple of minutes to relocate what had snagged his attention, then a couple more to figure out what it was.

Binoculars.

Someone was watching something through binoculars. Birdman shook as many of the cobwebs as he could out of what passed for his brain these days and tried to figure out what was going on. Staying one step ahead of trouble was his ticket to the survival train. Birdman wasn't big or strong, and he was basically scared of guns. His plan was to always stay one step ahead of the pack.

Daylight was coming fast, and he could make out two figures in the woods, not good enough to swear in court, but it looked like a man and a woman to him. Birdman followed their line of sight up the slope to the house. For a moment he wondered why they were spying on an ordinary, two-story white farmhouse that was probably close to a hundred years old. Then, at the edge of his vision, something moved. Birdman blinked and focused well enough to catch a glimpse of a man turning and walking toward the house. Something in the man's stride struck Birdman as familiar, but he was still too strung out to complete the connection.

Two

She was staring out the window as Davis stepped into the kitchen. The look on her face was one a person gets when their mind is drifting, and he wondered if she was remembering the past, or trying to see the future. Davis was never sure what his wife was thinking. He'd never really understood Ellen, or any woman for that matter. One way or another, they all were a mystery to him.

She turned her head, smiling. "Good morning."

"Morning. How you feeling today?"

"Not awful."

He sat his cup on the counter. Early last year they'd talked about replacing the Formica that had been there as far back as he could remember. Then Ellen had gotten sick and they'd never found the time or the energy to get started.

"Want a cup of tea?"

Ellen smiled again. It wasn't much of a smile. There wasn't any force behind it, but at least it was a smile.

"No thanks, I've already fixed myself one."

"Sure you felt up to that?"

"Davis, I'm not an invalid. I can still do lots for myself."

"I know, but..."

4

"But nothing. We've talked about this before, honey. I'll let you know when I need help, but I need to do things for myself when I can. Keep my strength up. You know what the doctors told us."

"When's your next treatment?" Davis didn't like to say the word 'chemo.' Just hearing it made his stomach queasy.

"Next Thursday. Will you be able to take me?"

He poured himself another cup of coffee and sipped. As it had aged, the coffee had acquired a bitter flavor. "I'll check my calendar when I get to the station."

He glanced at his watch. "Morning's getting away from me. I'd better be making tracks." He took a final sip, then placed the cup on the counter. "Want anything before I go?"

Ellen shook her head. "I'm good."

He crossed the floor, bent, and kissed her cheek. She smelled of medicine and, more faintly, of stale perfume. Some days he felt as though he could smell her flesh rotting from the cancer and all those harsh treatments the doctors ordered.

He thought about running his fingers through her hair—it was something he'd often done before the cancer—but decided against it. Her hair was so thin he could see the scalp underneath what remained. He wished for comforting words to say, but if there were any, they eluded him.

"Call me if you need me," he said, then turned on his heel and walked to the car without looking back. Once, he'd forgotten his badge and hadn't thought of it until he was halfway to the car, and when he'd walked back he'd found her sobbing. Since that day, Davis hadn't permitted himself to look back.

Three

"Morning, Sheriff."

Davis closed the door behind him and grinned at Claudia Miller. "Morning, Claudia. You doing okay this morning?"

She smiled. Claudia was a smiler...always pleasant, which he liked. Being pleasant made any day go better. Trouble was, his job often didn't allow much room for being pleasant.

"Doing fine, boss. And you?"

"Tolerable," he mumbled, then grinned to show he was doing some better than tolerable. "Coffee ready?"

"Yes, and you'd better grab a cup. Mayor's on the warpath this morning. Wants to see you as soon as you come in."

"What does he want this time?"

"He didn't say, but we had another overdose case last night."

Davis took a breath and let it out as he poured coffee into a Styrofoam cup. "Fatal?"

Claudia sighed. "Unfortunately. One of the Chisholm boys, is what I heard."

"Part of that bunch that lives out toward Bentley?"

"Nope, this one lived in West View. Somewhere on Cedar, if I got the story straight. Anyway, the mayor is really upset. You'd best drink your coffee and go see him."

The Chisholm name nagged at Davis for a second, then the synapses shifted and he felt his guts go cold. He didn't say anything, merely sipped his coffee. Claudia was right, he'd have to go see the mayor, even though he didn't want to. When he got upset, the mayor always seemed to lose his temper and start shouting. A shouting match before lunch wasn't exactly on Davis' morning agenda.

Still, he'd recognized the name. Maybe it wasn't the same kid he knew, but the odds were good it was. He'd been a good kid when Davis had known him.

"Anything else happening?"

Claudia studied the notes on her desk. "Not much. Couple of DUIs last night and you need to work on the monthly expense reports."

"Oh boy." Davis turned and went out the door he'd just entered. "Going to see the mayor," he said over his shoulder.

Four

Mary Green was guarding the mayor as usual. She looked up from the *West View Chronicle* spread across her desk. It was open to the crossword puzzle.

"Claudia said he wanted to see me."

Mary eyed him over the top of her glasses. "That's right. He's been expecting you."

Davis checked his watch. "Pretty early for him to be in the office, isn't it?"

Mary snorted. "Mayor Gregory is a hard worker."

"So," he said, "it's still early for him."

The woman glared and pursed her lips like she was going to say something. Davis glared back. He'd never cared much for Mary Green. She was a bit too stuck on herself, especially when she wasn't overly blessed with brains or beauty. She'd been one grade behind Davis in school, and, simply because she looked cute in her cheerleader outfit, he'd asked her out. She had snubbed him, but good. Remembering incidents like that was one thing he was good at. He took another sip of coffee and pointed at the closed inner door.

"You want to let him know I'm here, or should I just go on in?"

"I'll let him know." She turned her head, picked up the phone and pressed a button. Following a brief whispered conversation, she lifted her eyes and jabbed her chin at the door. "You can knock and go on in."

Davis tilted his head back as he drained the last of the coffee. Then he set the empty cup on Mary's desk, an act that earned him another glare.

He winked at the woman—just to piss her off—squared his shoulders and started walking. He rapped the door once and swung it open.

Ed Gregory was staring at him from the far side of his desk. "I was going to say come in, but looks like I can save my vocal cords the bother."

"You wanted to see me?"

"Yes, indeed." Gregory made a sweeping motion with his left arm that ended with the fingers pointing at one of the two chairs in front of his desk.

"I'm good."

The mayor shrugged. "Suit yourself." He studied the top of his desk for a minute, then took an audible breath and lifted his eyes.

"You heard about the Chisholm boy?"

Davis nodded. He'd learned a long time ago it was usually better to talk less and listen more, especially around Ed Gregory.

"He was only nineteen. Would have turned twenty next week. His dad and I are in the Lodge together."

So what, was Davis' first thought, but he kept his mouth shut. Instead, he assumed what he hoped was a suitably stern expression.

"Davis, this was a good kid. Made all-conference in baseball last spring. Rumor was the Royals were looking at him."

"I knew him some. He had talent."

"You knew him, huh?"

"If he's the kid I'm thinking of, I did. Helped Paul Dixon coach the American Legion a couple of years ago and he was one of the pitchers. Nice kid."

If the dead boy was the Mark Chisholm Davis had coached, he was a tall lefty with a really good curve and a slider. His fastball hadn't been great, but it had been good enough. Plus, he'd been a nice kid, seventeen or eighteen, young enough to still have a certain innocence about him. A kid with a future. Davis hadn't figured him for drugs, but his batting average along the prognostication lines wouldn't have moved him up from Double A.

"I'm sure that's him. You played some ball yourself back in the day, didn't you, Davis?"

"Some."

"Heard you were real good."

"Let's say better than average. Mostly Triple A. Cup of coffee with the Cardinals."

"Really? I hadn't heard that."

"It wasn't much. I was no Hall of Famer. My curve ball didn't break enough. Only pitched in four games with St. Louis late one season when they were out of the race. All the games were on the west coast. Tore my rotator cuff against the Dodgers. And that was the end."

"Tough."

Yeah, Davis thought, real tough, but not as tough as dying young.

Davis massaged the back of his neck. "Heard it was heroin."

"That's what Fred thinks."

Davis processed the information. Fred Hill was the local coroner and, with all the overdoses the past few months, he probably had a real good idea of what had happened.

"Said it was probably laced with fentanyl." Gregory shook his head. "So much of that lately. Way too much."

He paused then, as though he expected Davis to commiserate, or jump up and down, or something along those lines. Sure, he hated to hear the news. Nobody needed to go out like that, especially a good kid like Mark. But drugs were so prevalent in Pratt County, the state of Missouri for that matter, that it was beyond the forces of one small sheriff's office to control. Besides, West View had its own police force. Where was Chief Evans, anyway?

"Heard the boy lived on Cedar."

"That's right. Just three houses down from me."

"Doesn't that make it a city matter?"

The mayor made a face. "Not really. Mark died out on the far side of Black Creek. That throws it square in your boat. Judge Peel had to go to Kansas City this morning. He asked me to let you know. Besides, Chief Evans is down a couple of officers. Kleinschmidt quit last week."

"Where's he going?"

"Independence."

"More money?"

"Hundred dollars a week more." Gregory shook his head again. "It's getting so we get somebody trained and they get a year of experience, why then Kansas City or Springfield or Independence makes them an offer we can't match. All we're left with is a greenhorn or some joker with a black mark on his record. Or somebody who's over the hill."

Davis tried not to let anything show, but something must have changed in his face. Or maybe Gregory realized what he'd inferred.

"Sorry," he said, "nothing personal."

"Don't worry about it." It wasn't the mayor's fault fifty had recently slid in the rearview mirror for Davis. "What do you want to me to do?"

"Look into this for me, Davis. Personally. I knew Mark, you see. He was a good kid. Had all his life in front of him...Well, you know what I mean."

Davis knew what he meant, all right. And Mark had deserved better. But this was the sort of case he didn't like. Ninety percent of them led nowhere. But he'd do it, partly because it was his job, and partly because he'd known Mark, seen him win, and lose, heard him cuss and laugh and cry. But he'd do it his way. Davis didn't like doing favors. Once you did one for somebody, they seemed to think they had some sort of claim on you.

He glanced out the window. A black pickup was rolling down the street. Outside the post office, the flag hung limp. He took a deep breath and let it out, keeping his eyes on the street. "I'll drive out there and take a look around. Probably won't amount to much. There's so much of that shit floating around, it will be damn near impossible to find out where he got it."

The mayor rearranged his face. "That's where we may have caught a break. Mark's girlfriend said he'd told her that he was getting the heroin locally."

"West View? Pratt County?"

"Locally, was all she told Officer Smith."

Davis tugged a small notebook out of his shirt pocket. "What's her name?"

"Karen Ross."

"Phone number?"

"I don't know. You ought to be able to get it from the police report."

"Yep," Davis said and turned and walked out, without looking at either Gregory or Mary Green. He didn't mean to be rude. It was more that his mind was on a young lefthander who'd had a real fine curve, one he'd never throw again. That pissed Davis off.

Five

"Heard from Tommy this morning?"

Claudia Miller smiled over the top of her teacup. "He clocked out ten minutes ago. Now, I don't know for sure, but he usually grabs breakfast over at the City Café when he comes off the night shift."

"You know where I'll be." Davis turned and walked back out into the morning.

The sun was up over the rooftops, coating the street and the buildings with light. Blinking against the sudden brightness, he started walking west. A block and half down, on the same side of Main Street, he pushed open the door to one of the two restaurants in West View. Twenty years ago, there had been five, six if you counted the counter at Farley Drugs. Now there were only two. Things change, the sheriff thought, but not always for the better.

A mixed aroma of bacon cooking and coffee brewing greeted him as he let his eyes wander around the café. There was a better crowd than he'd expected. Most of the customers were men, but a few women were scattered among the tables. He knew several of the men and a couple of the women. He spotted his deputy at a table in the far corner, smiled at Earlene Dixon, who was seated as usual behind the cash register, and crossed the café.

Sunlight poured in through the windows and his shadow floated on ahead, then fell across a plate of eggs and bacon. The eggs were sunny side up, the bacon was nearly black. His stomach growled. "Care if I join you?"

The deputy casually saluted and smiled. "No, sir. Got an extra chair right here. Besides, I could use the company."

Sheriff Wells sat down and a waitress sidled over. She was young, blonde, and thin, and he had no clue who she was. Lots of newcomers in Pratt County these days. Too many for one old sheriff to keep up with.

"What'll you have this morning?"

"Coffee. Black."

"Nothing to eat?"

"Nope."

"Suit yourself." The girl whirled and started for the kitchen. Davis watched her walk away. She had a smooth easy stride, a way of walking that Ellen had when they first met.

He rubbed at his face, noting he'd not done much of a job of shaving.

"Not hungry, boss?"

"Naw, ate before I left home."

"How's your wife?"

"Said she was having a good day."

The deputy forked eggs into his mouth. "That's great," he mumbled around the eggs.

"Suppose so."

The girl came back and set a cup of coffee down in front of Davis. Her name tag read Nevaeh. What the hell kind of name was that? Parents sure picked strange names these days. He peered down at his coffee. Dark and thick, it put him in mind of boiling mud. He blew across the liquid, then raised the cup to his lips. The coffee tasted like it looked. Putting the cup down, he eyed his deputy. The man looked real young to him, but these days so many people did. He supposed it was just the generations changing. He had to smile at himself. Once, he'd been the young kid in the tight-fitting uniform.

"Heard you had an OD last night."

Deputy Smith stopped chewing and made a face. "Yeah, way out on Black Creek, just past where the old grocery store stood. You know where the creek makes a bend south?"

"Yes."

"Well, I was patrolling out there, and about a hundred yards beyond that bend, I saw this car on the side of the road with its lights off, only the engine was still running. Figured I'd better check it out. At first, I didn't think anybody was inside. But when I shone my flashlight on the back seat, there he was, leaning against the door on the driver's side—sort of half sitting and half lying down."

"Alive?"

"Deader than a hammer."

"Been dead long?"

Deputy Smith grimaced. "He wasn't cold, yet, but he wasn't ninety-eight point six either. Fred Hill said he figured the boy had been gone for close to an hour."

"Mayor said Fred thought it was heroin."

"Probably was. I found some residue and that's what it looked like. Laced with fentanyl is my guess. Same as what killed that girl at Lake Pimlico last week."

"Yeah, I remember." The bell above the door jingled and a fat man in a rumpled suit stepped into the café. Davis recognized him—one of the attorneys in town—but couldn't come up with his name. He was getting bad about that. Forgetting things wasn't good. That was the way it had started for his mother.

He sipped his coffee again. Cooling hadn't done a thing for the taste. "What brand of vehicle?"

The deputy pushed his cap back, then rubbed at his forehead like he was trying to warm up his memory. "White Camry, maybe three, four years old."

"Run the plate?"

"That's how I knew for sure who it was. Thought I recognized him, but the way it took him, his face was all twisted up."

"That's the way it happens for some. Mayor said it was a kid from town. Mark Chisholm."

"Yep, turns out I did know him. He was a couple of grades behind me in school. Think he was a freshman when I was a senior. Good baseball player, if I'm remembering right."

"Yeah, he was hot stuff." Davis looked away, out into the street and on to the antique store on the other side. Hell, he felt like an antique this morning. He started to say that out loud, then changed his mind.

"See anything out of the ordinary? Anything that might give us some clue as to where he got the stuff? Or who he got it from?"

Deputy Smith wiped egg yolk off the corner of his mouth while he studied the question. A UPS truck rumbled down the street. Somebody in the booth behind them started laughing.

The deputy shook his head and grinned as he pulled a small piece of notebook paper out of his shirt pocket and unfolded it. "Not unless an empty Diet Coke can, a Kansas City parking ticket, a wrapped peppermint, a Bank of West View pen that doesn't write, a battered baseball, a book on the life of Warren Spahn, or a red, white, and blue hair barrette signifies."

Davis took a final slug of coffee, made a face and stood up. "Thanks, Tommy. Guess I'd better go start digging." The man in the next booth laughed again and Davis tossed a dollar bill down on the table, turned and walked for the door, trying to remember when he'd last laughed out loud.

Six

This time Birdman came out of the sleep curve wide awake, ready to start moving. As usual, his first thought centered on where he was going to score his next fix. Then he opened his eyes to see where he was.

He looked up into a sea of grass, waving in a gentle breeze. An unseen bird trilled at him and sunlight spray-painted his face. Birdman sat up.

Now that his line of sight was above the waving grasses, he took a good look around. To the west, he could see nothing beyond more grass. Looking south, he could see a line of fence, with a glimpse of a paved road just beyond. Birdman twisted around and stared east. He could make out one corner of a barn and a small stock pond, half hidden by weeping willows. Frustrated, Birdman struggled to his feet and peered north. At last, he thought, a house. Unfortunately, he didn't recognize it. Well, he'd done it again, Birdman told himself, as he tried to decide what to do.

His mind wasn't functioning on all cylinders and it took him a couple of minutes to decide he'd better start walking. Halfway to the road, he remembered seeing the figures in the trees and then the man standing on the grassy knoll. Something about that man worried the mind of Birdman, but not enough synapses were functioning yet and the memory wouldn't come. By the time he made the pavement, sweat dampened the back of his shirt and beaded his face.

Seven

Fred Hill smoked cigars. Damn nasty cigars, although Sheriff Wells couldn't blame the man. If he had to spend most of his time dealing with dead bodies, he'd probably be smoking cigars, too. Or something stronger. The death stench alone made him half-nauseous. Not that he'd seen all that many, maybe a couple of dozen since he'd been on the job, but they all shared one thing—the uniquely disturbing aroma that foretold death.

"We'll have to wait on the toxicology reports, Davis, but I'll bet you lunch at Applebee's it was heroin laced with fentanyl."

Davis was leaning against a wall, breathing shallow and studying the lifeline in his left hand. "What makes you say that?"

"I've seen so many lately I'm starting to be able to predict." Hill stuck his cigar back in his mouth and began puffing. "Could be wrong, of course." He winked. "Am occasionally, you know. Still, I doubt it this time. This makes the third one this month and we've still got a week left in June."

"Where do they get that shit?"

"Hell, Sheriff, finding that out is your job."

"I know, I know. But we shut one dealer down and two more pop up in his place. Or maybe her place. We're starting to see the women selling, too. You heard about that Whitlow girl from Carter Point?"

"Just what I read in the paper."

"Well, she was running a real operation. Had four or five high school kids selling, or at least delivering, for her. Not that she was old by any stretch. Think she was twenty-two, maybe twenty-three. Good looking girl, too. Understand she'd been a majorette in high school."

Hill tugged the cigar out of his mouth. "How'd you catch her?"

"Undercover agent. Made three buys trying to get a handle on her network. Nailed her on the third. Figured we'd better move before she slipped out of state on us."

A memory of Kansas slow danced across his mind—a hot, windy summer day in Hays, with the wind blowing down the streets like they were tunnels and it was a zephyr headed for Kentucky. Sunlight was blistering anything it touched. He'd been a young man then. Younger, anyway, full of hopes, dreams, and wishes. Now, he sure knew where wishing got you.

Davis pushed off the wall. "Gotta run, Fred. Lots of criminals running around loose, you know." He grinned. "Thanks."

Fred waved the business end of his cigar in Davis' direction. Davis flung up a hand as he walked out the door.

Eight

Lawton Turner leaned against the shadow darkened wall of the Pratt County History Museum. A Royals baseball cap shaded his face, sunglasses covered his eyes, and a Marlboro dangled from his lips. An inch or two over six feet, Turner was slim and lean-hipped, but muscles in his arms bunched like corded rope.

Turner took a drag off his cigarette and blew smoke out his nostrils. A blue jay fussed at him from the top branch of a twisted cedar, but Turner ignored the bird. His eyes swept across the street that ran before him, shifted between the sidewalks on either side of the street, drifted across the people coming out of the buildings, exiting their cars, or strolling down the sidewalk.

For several minutes, his only movement was to occasionally pull the cigarette from between his lips, then replace it. At 10:47, he straightened, leaning almost imperceptibly forward, his eyes fixed on another man, one walking briskly toward a pickup truck with the words *Pratt County Sheriff* scripted on the door.

Turner tossed his cigarette to the ground, then rubbed his right boot across it. He cocked his head, eyeing the second man as he entered the vehicle. Lawton Turner's eyes followed the truck as it rolled out of town, his lips curled in a grimace masquerading as a smile.

Nine

Normally, he liked driving the backroads. Patrolling in Pratt County didn't often amount to more than driving around the countryside, enjoying the scenery. In the six years he'd been sheriff, Davis Wells could count on the fingers of his hands the times he'd actually come on a crime in progress.

Oh, it happened. Like when he happened to be driving by the Fast Stop just outside Drayton and saw the Farley boys breaking in the side door. But, for most of his time in office, he'd worked days and there sure wasn't a lot going on then, at least not many break-ins, holdups, or drunken fist fights. Sure, there was criminal activity in the daytime, crimes like speeding and DUI and shoplifting, but the night was where the real action was. These days, Davis did a lot of night patrols. Only trouble was, he wasn't always looking for crime after dark. Many nights he simply wanted to be alone, away from the odors of sickness.

Unconsciously, he'd come the long way. Instead of swinging halfway around the country, he should have simply driven east on Highway P. Maybe, he considered, his brain was slipping. He rolled by the white frame church at Newton, twisted the wheel and headed out H, going west toward West View. The radio was squawking, but the chatter was routine and Davis powered the window down to let the air blow across the cabin of the truck. It carried with it the scents of freshly turned earth, fertilizer, and something sweet blooming.

The blacktop went up a rise, then bent south on the downside, flattened out and ran straight for a quarter mile before it went up another rise. When he reached the crest, Black Creek and the bridge were both visible. On the far side of the bridge was a splash of yellow police tape, and Mark Chisholm's car. Davis pressed the brake, coasted across the bridge and past the car, before pulling over onto a wide, grassy spot next to the creek.

He cut the engine and sat listening to the engine ping and the ripple of water sliding over rocks. Slowly, a mockingbird began tuning up and Davis popped the door and swung his legs out of the truck. Heat was starting to build and he could feel sweat forming under his uniform as he pushed out of the cab and began walking toward the car.

He didn't really expect to find anything, but he'd learned a long time ago it was always better to follow protocol, be thorough, and never take any shortcuts, if you could help it.

There wasn't anything special about the car, at least at first glance. It was a fairly new Toyota, the basic Camry, white, none too clean. The driver's window was down and the left rear quarter panel was dented. Davis walked around the car, letting his eyes wander, trying to pick up something that stood out, that didn't necessarily belong—a cigarette butt, a piece of paper, tire tread that didn't match the tires on the Camry.

He kept circling, tightening the circuit the second time, seeing nothing out of the ordinary except for a small garter snake as it slithered off into a patch of tall grass. Officer Smith had already bagged all the items he'd found inside the car, but a second look wouldn't hurt. Besides, Smith hadn't been on the job long and only experience really taught a cop what to look for. Finding a book on Warren Spahn was fine, but there might have been a hair, or a raveling, even a key that had been overlooked. Davis opened the driver's door and leaned into the cabin. He owed the Chisholm kid that much.

A faint odor greeted him. Actually, it was an amalgamation of odors—sweat, dust, and dried urine—and a dozen others so tightly swirled together it would have taken a scientist to separate them. Maybe it was because he knew Mark Chisholm had died in the vehicle, but it seemed that the mingling of all those scents signified death. Davis shook his head and bent down, trying to see if anything was under the driver's seat.

It took twenty minutes to cover the entire cabin of the vehicle. After all that, he didn't have much to show for his time and trouble: one section of the protective covering on a Band-Aid, a plastic water bottle top, a swirly blue hair-barrette, a dirty nickel, some crumbs that might have been almost anything, and a single, long strand of hair. The hair was either blue or black, depending on how the light hit it. He placed each item in a separate bag and started for his vehicle. Halfway there, he heard the whine of an engine and turned in time to see one of his deputies rolling for the bridge.

By the time the cruiser made the bridge, Davis could see Hensley was driving. Hensley was one of the old hands, old being the key word. Hensley was older than he was, which made him an ancient cop. Middle age wasn't what it was cracked up to be—all that prime of life shit and other lies. Since he'd turned fifty, Davis felt the days like iron on his shoulders. Yet, he could also sense them slipping away. Time seemed to flow faster every year. He turned to greet Hensley.

"Hey, boss."

"What's up, Willie?"

"You're a wanted man."

"What are you rambling about?"

"Mayor wants you. Called the office and said he'd been trying to reach you. Only your cell phone goes straight to voice mail and you've got the radio turned off."

"So?"

Hensley chuckled. "So, the mayor wants to talk to you, like right away. In his office. He called down to the station and told me to find you and tell you to come to his office as soon as you can."

Davis pushed his cap back and rubbed his forehead. "What's the mayor's problem?"

"Mayor didn't say, only indicated real clear that he wanted you in his office as soon as I could make that happen." He turned and spat a brown stream. "Now, I did see that Chisholm boy's daddy in the waiting room..." Hensley's voice tailed off and he scuffed his boots in the roadside dust.

A crow cawed in a sycamore across the creek and the two men turned to look. The crow was rocking back and forth on a bare limb three-fourths of the way up. Davis pointed at the bird, then let his gaze wander up a slight rise of ground. A stand of maples grew along the crest and a light breeze fluttered their leaves. Above the trees, the sky was high and had the appearance of baked enamel. For a moment he thought again about moving to Kansas. Thinking about what you couldn't have was hard, he told himself. Hard and stupid.

Davis turned toward Hensley. "Tell the mayor I'll be along when I finish my examination of the crime scene."

A fly buzzed Hensley's face and he brushed it away. "Mayor Gregory said to be sure and tell you he wanted you to come and see him right away."

The sheriff didn't say anything. He could hear cattle off in the distance and smell honeysuckle somewhere close. For a moment he thought about Ellen, then he thought about Mark Chisholm's body lying cold and rotting in the morgue. His mind seemed to shift with the wind.

Hensley coughed, and Davis tugged the visor of his cap down tighter. "Willie, you tell the mayor that my dad always told me people in hell want ice water."

Hensley grinned, gave the sheriff a sloppy salute, turned, and strolled back to his cruiser. He looked thin in the sunlight, thin and weather beaten, but Davis knew his deputy was a helluva lot tougher than he first appeared.

Tough, that's what a man had to be these days if he wanted to make it, Davis thought. Especially when the walls started closing in.

Ten

"Davis, this is Dave Chisholm, Mark's father."

The man rose slowly from his chair, turning his face toward Davis, letting a small, soft sound escape. He was lean, wiry looking—a man who kept in shape, or was trying to. Davis had seen him before, in the stands at ball games. If the man remembered Davis, he didn't show it. He extended his hand. "Sheriff."

"Mr. Chisholm, I'm sorry about your son."

"Thank you, but what are you doing about it?"

Davis propped his butt on a round table the mayor sometimes used for meetings. "We're following procedure. One of my deputies has been over the crime scene, and I'm just back from taking a look myself. We've found a few items we'll get analyzed while we're waiting for the autopsy report. We'll do some interviews to see if anybody close to Mark has any ideas for us."

Chisholm stared him straight in the eyes. Something in his stare caused Davis to figure him for tougher than the average bear. Chisholm started to say something, then paused as he swallowed. He looked like he was trying to choke down a rock. Licking his lips, he tried again. "Do you have any leads?"

Davis made sure he kept his eyes fixed on the dead boy's father, knowing he would have appreciated that if the roles had been reversed. "Too early to say, Mr. Chisholm. Like I mentioned, we've found a few items in your son's car we need to follow-up on. Now, one or two of them may prove to be a real clue, or not. Just can't say at this point."

"You said you've found some things, Sheriff. What kinds of things?"

"Sorry, Mr. Chisholm, but at this juncture I can't discuss the case. If it turns out to be something other than an accident, I don't want to show our hand."

"But it's my son who's dead. Doesn't that count?"

Davis rubbed his face with the palm of his left hand. Talking to a parent right after their child had died was hell. Murder, accident, suicide, it didn't matter. The death of a child was never pleasant; there was never any damn good in it.

"Sure, that matters, Mr. Chisholm. But it's not a good idea to let anyone know what evidence, or potential evidence, the police have. Don't want to give away the game, see?"

Chisholm took a deep breath like he was planning to let loose a rampage of words, but, before he could get rolling, the mayor rose from behind his desk and cleared his throat. "Now, Davis..."

"Sorry," Davis said, pushing off the table. "I've got evidence in my vehicle and need to get started on that." He sure didn't need to hear Gregory spewing hot wind. He nodded at Chisholm. "Good to see you again, Mr. Chisholm. Sorry it had to be under these circumstances."

Chisholm nodded back and Davis turned and headed for the door. The mayor was talking, but he wasn't listening. Thoughts and images of all the dead he'd seen were swirling around his brain. So many dead faces made him half-dizzy. He shook his head to clear them and pulled the door open.

Davis drove back to the office where he spent an hour signing forms and going through the files. He made a couple of calls about Mark Chisholm, but all he learned was that the kid had signed a contract with the Royals and been assigned to their Burlington club, and that he was scheduled to report in two days.

Outside, the day was growing old. Davis knew that feeling. The phone call had put a year on his age. Just thinking about a kid with so much future being dead pissed the hell out of him. He locked his desk, waved at Claudia on his way out, and headed for the truck. He needed a drink, but he needed to get home, too. Home won, this time.

Eleven

Sunlight stretched across the land, a radiant golden blanket covering the earth. A breeze had come up in the last hour, and the pasture grasses shimmered in their ancient, natural dance. A brown thrasher swooped down and settled on the white picket fence that fronted the yard, swaying gently as it cocked its head and eyed the sky.

Ellen Wells saw none of this. She didn't hear the rustle of leaves of the maple that had been dying since she and Davis had married and moved to the farm. She didn't smell the fresh turned earth at the Groves' place where it met their property. She didn't feel the wooden arm of the porch swing worn smooth by three generations of her husband's family.

Her oblivion to life outside her body was intense, total. Her focus was internal, her mind searching for any answer to the evil slowly cannibalizing her body. No, slowly was not *le mot juste*, as Rayford Roth, her linguistics teacher at the University of Central Missouri, would have said. Perhaps iniquitous was the better word choice. For the cancer that had been feasting on her for over a year was indeed grossly unfair and morally wrong.

What, she asked herself repeatedly, had she done to deserve such an invasion? Hadn't she always tried to live a good life, to follow the golden rule? Well, maybe not so much in the seventh grade, or that time Adelle Simpkins had helped herself to Ellen's paper on the sonnets of William Shakespeare. But, all in all, for over fifty years, she'd tried to live the way she'd been taught: by her parents, society, the Bible. She'd tried, with great diligence, to be a good daughter, wife, mother, friend. And what had all that effort, all those sacrifices got her?

Cancer.

Some rare cancer of the blood, a disease that affected one in a million, a curse that was killing her. That, an estranged son, a husband who spent more hours every week on the job, and a body that was betraying her.

She despised herself when she cried, although she cried virtually every day. So, when the tears became too many for her tired eyes to hold, she said two very bad words, which perfectly summed up her anguish, and her anger, pushed out of the swing, maneuvered down the steps through the tears, and began to walk.

By the time she made the mailbox, the shadows had begun to lengthen and stretch their arms across the highway, and she knew her husband would be coming home soon. So she dried her tears, fussed with her hair, bit her lip, turned, and retraced her footsteps.

It was time for her to cook supper. Even in her season of sorrow, duty called, and Ellen always did her best to answer. Intuition, or instinct, told her that made her stronger. And she had to stay strong. Cancer never quit. Well, there was no law that said she had to quit either.

Cry a few tears, then go on. That was the way she saw her path unfolding. Her husband thought she was an invalid. Dammit, but he was wrong about her—and not for the first time, she told herself. She intended to show him just how wrong.

Her legs were tired now, and it was a chore to catch her breath. That was all right. A cup of tea, and five minutes in the old rocker that stood before the south window and she'd be fine again—for long enough to fix supper, anyway.

Twelve

The cicadas had been humming for a week and their constant noise was getting on Davis' nerves. It felt like his eardrums were vibrating. Putting his fork down, he studied his wife.

She was stirring mashed potatoes on her plate, swirling her fork around and around and around. Her eyes weren't on her plate, though. She was looking past the table, across the kitchen, out the window to somewhere distant, somewhere only she could go. He didn't know where it was, but he was sure it wasn't Kansas. Her gaze never wavered as she kept stirring. Swirl, swirl, swirl went the fork as the cicadas kept humming. His mind was trying to go places he didn't want it to. Davis started silently counting the fork swirls. When the count reached thirty, he said, "You okay?"

His wife's eyes blinked, and he watched her come back into the kitchen. "Sorry, what did you say?"

"I asked if you were okay."

She smiled. "I'm fine," she said. She appeared tired to him—real tired, bone tired.

"You look tired and you've not touched a thing on your plate."

"I was thinking."

"About what?"

Her lips rearranged themselves and she said, "Nothing, really."

"Oh, come on, Ellen, nobody simply sits around stirring mashed potatoes on their plate and thinking of nothing. You had to be thinking of something. You can't think of just nothing."

"But I really wasn't thinking of anything in particular. I was merely letting thoughts roll across my mind."

"Like tumbleweeds, I suppose?"

"Yes, that's it. Like tumbleweeds."

Davis jabbed a piece of ham in his mouth and started chewing. He was never was sure when to keep probing and when to shut up. If he didn't ask, she said he didn't care. If he did ask, she said he was being nosy, that she needed her private space. Private space he could understand. He liked privacy as well as the next person, maybe better. Still, he couldn't seem to win with Ellen these days. Of course, she had cancer and the treatments had been terrible. The cancer—that had been the start of the really bad, hard times. But nothing was finished. Every damn thing was hanging out there, loose and flapping, blowing in the wind.

Half-assed, his dad would have called it, and right then a longing to see his father one more time rose in him until his brain hurt like he'd been smashed by a hammer. Hurt so bad that for a second it felt like he was having a heart attack. Then he swallowed the ham he'd been chewing, picked up his coffee cup, pushed out of his chair, and walked to the kitchen window.

As Davis sipped the cooling coffee, he gazed out across the side yard, past the huge stump where the great American elm had stood when he'd been a boy, past the remnants of the garden his father had raised, and his father before him, down the slope toward the D.C. Groves place. D.C. was the last of the old timers, men who had actually known his father, and he had to be eighty if he was a day. From the window, Davis couldn't see the road that ran behind the Groves' yard, and he sure couldn't see Kansas. But still, he wished he were there.

In his mind, he could see Hays, Kansas on a summer day. Davis pictured himself standing in the shade of the Midwest Bank, leaning against the warm bricks, with the hot wind that had started in some flat wheat field a hundred miles away blowing across his face, and the sweat sliding down his back, watching the farmers saunter by in their overalls, the businessmen in their coats and ties, the women in their sunglasses and summer blouses, and the kids running and laughing, chasing one another in spite of the heat. And the best thing was, the absolute best thing, he didn't know a soul, and not one person, not one lousy person knew him. He didn't know their names, or their Uncle George, or where they went to school or church, or where they lived or worked, and, best of all, he didn't know any of the sins they'd committed, and they didn't know his.

"Eat your supper, Ellen," he said, turning from the window, and Kansas, and peace of mind. "Eat your supper. You need your strength. Besides, I've got to go back out tonight."

"But you worked all day." Ellen turned then, looking at him, her eyes sliding across the contours of his face.

"Afraid so. It's that Chisholm boy, the one that died over on Black Creek. Mayor and the boy's dad are both raising seven kinds of hell, really pushing me. I've got to get rolling before they get the wrong idea."

Ellen opened her mouth like she was going to say something. In the end, however, she didn't say a word. Merely gave him a searching look, turned her face away, and stared down at her plate.

Davis drained his coffee and set his cup in the sink. Then he crossed the room and turned the radio on, twisting the dial until he found a station playing dance music. Dance music his mother and dad might have danced to. He stacked the dirty dishes in the dishpan, squeezed in dishwashing liquid and turned on the hot water, pushing the faucet to the side until the water came out hot.

She was eating now. Only small bites, a dab of mashed potatoes, or peas, a bite of ham now and then, chewing slowly, rhythmically. While the water was heating, Davis watched her eat. There were words he wanted to say, but he didn't think they would do any good. Sometimes talk wasn't the answer.

He crossed the floor and stood behind her. She stiffened, but didn't turn around. Davis stroked her hair. Before, it had been soft and long, now it was short and brittle. He knew things changed, people changed, only not often for the better. Life did it to every man, woman, and child—changed them. He figured the water was hot by then, so he spun on a heel and quickstepped to the sink. When the soap suds started sliding over the sides of the dishpan, he turned the water off.

The song on the radio changed then, and, while the dishes were soaking, Davis started putting the leftover food in the refrigerator. He'd do the dishes, he thought, and maybe watch a game show with Ellen. Then he had to go. After that, he had to go.

Thirteen

The name of the bar was Missouri Wet and it was like every other bar Davis had ever been in. The lighting was dim, the jukebox was several decibels too loud, and it smelled of beer and stale sweat, along with a montage of perfumes and aftershaves. He'd stopped in a few times before, and, when he stepped up to the bar, the bartender, who was a former high school history teacher, leaned over and said, "The usual, Davis?"

"That'll work, Rudy."

The bartender poured a generous shot of Knob Creek and eased it down in front of Davis. "Wanna run a tab tonight?"

"No thanks, don't plan on being here long. Should be a one-and-done evening." Davis handed the bartender a twenty, and the man stacked Davis' change on the polished wood.

"Heard about that Chisholm boy. That's a damn shame."

"That it is."

"Played baseball, didn't he?"

"Yes." Davis said, letting his eyes drift away. He didn't want to be rude, but he didn't want to talk about a dead nineteen-year-old who was supposed to report to the Burlington Royals in two days.

Rudy wasn't the best at taking a hint. "If I remember right, he played for the American Legion team when you were coaching."

"Yeah, that's right."

"Good kid, wasn't he?"

"Yep," Davis said, picking up his drink and glancing at Rudy. "Mark was a good kid, a real good kid."

Rudy looked like he was aiming to say something else, but Davis started working his way toward an empty table in the far corner.

The jukebox was playing what passed for a country song these days. It sounded bland as hell to Davis, but then he was an old man by music standards—give him Ernest Tubb or Don Gibson or Hank Snow any day.

Davis tilted his chair against the wall and watched the action through slitted eyes. For a weeknight, the place was hopping. All the stools along the bar were filled, mostly with men, but there were a few single women, plus several couples at the tables. The jukebox switched to a slow song and three couples got up to dance. Davis thought about when he and Ellen used to slow dance. A dancer he never would be, but he could shuffle around the floor well enough if the song were slow enough and Ellen would let him hold her tight enough. But he wasn't dancing tonight, so he sipped his bourbon and watched other people dancing.

Whenever he went to a bar, he always ended up wondering why he had come. Because bars tended to be dark and full of strangers, Davis figured he came to get away from work and home, and he supposed he also came because he thought he might be able to drown a few of the tensions that were twisting inside his guts like barbed wire. But, in the end, things never turned out quite like he hoped they would and he always left mad at himself.

The music transitioned to an upbeat tune, and several couples got up to dance, including a middle-aged overweight couple who joined a raggedy line-dance formation. The couple put Davis in mind of a pair of hogs up on their hind legs trying to walk. Time for him to leave.

Davis lifted the glass and slugged about a third of it down. He let that burn for a moment, then lifted the glass again. One more swallow, he told himself, then head for the house. He closed his eyes.

The scent of lilacs was the first hint. Then Davis felt a strand of hair brush across his cheek, followed by the laying on of smooth, soft hands. Davis opened his eyes.

He'd never seen her before, but she leaned in and smiled. "Hi, thought you looked lonely, and I am lonely, so I thought I'd join you. If that's okay?"

He should have said no. Part of him even wanted to say no. Davis knew better than to say yes. If he'd said no, a helluva lot of lives might have played out differently. But the woman he'd never seen before was right—he was lonely, and he was tired, and it had been a damn long time since he'd been with a woman who was smiling at him. So, Davis patted the empty chair next to his, and she squeezed his arm and sat.

"Hi, my name is Tanya."

"Mine's Davis. What are you drinking?"

"How about a margarita?"

Davis signaled for the waitress, and, while he was giving her the order, took a look around the room, hoping none of the faces was familiar. If anybody he knew was there, he'd have to tell them he was on a case. Fortunately, the lighting wasn't much, and he only saw one face that struck him as even halfway familiar.

"You from around here, Davis?"

"I live a few miles away." The waitress brought the margarita and Davis paid. Tanya lifted her glass, closed her eyes, and took a long sip. Davis took the opportunity to study her face. It was pretty in an elongated, thin way—a face Modigliani might have painted. It was too dark to tell the color of her eyes and all he could tell about her hair was that it was long and dark. Desire to stroke it drove him back to his drink.

"I live out in the county, too. Kinda close to East Point. Know the town?"

"Been there a few times."

She stroked his arm. Her hand felt like a velvet glove sliding up and down. "What sort of work do you do, Davis?"

Davis wasn't sure if he wanted to answer that question, for a number of reasons. Before he could make up his mind, the music switched to something slow, with saxophones, and he smiled at the woman with velvet hands and asked her if she wanted to dance.

She rose smoothly, and Davis steered them to a shadowy corner where they slow danced in an elliptical orbit. She nestled her head against his chest so that her hair was in his face and her breath was warm against his skin. She smelled of lilacs. He kissed the top of her head and wanted to do more. Davis told himself he was a married man, but then he told himself a lot of things. Her body seemed to mold to his, and Davis felt himself respond. He kept hoping the song would end soon, at the same time wishing it never had to end.

When the music changed, Davis disengaged and walked her back to the table. He was sweating, and was glad the lighting was lousy. He was also grateful for the modicum of self-discipline he had managed to maintain.

Davis made a show of looking at his watch. "Hate to rush, but it's getting late and I've got to work in the morning. Expect I'd better say good-bye."

"So soon?"

"It's getting on for midnight."

"Oh, is it that late?" She put a hand on his left arm. "Would you mind to walk me to my car?"

"Sure," he said, "let's go."

They walked out together, not touching, but close—like an old married couple. Davis tried damn hard not to think about Ellen.

Outside the bar, cool air felt good against his face. The parking lot was full and she'd had to park in the gravel overflow lot. The crunch of gravel beneath their feet sounded like tiny lightbulbs popping. The moon was playing hide and seek behind the clouds and a faint breeze carried scents of fertilizer, cattle, and honeysuckle.

She stopped at a Chevy near the east end of the gravel, next to a ragged line of second growth trees. Their shadows covered her car and their faces. She turned hers up to his.

"Nice to meet you, Davis."

"Nice to meet you."

"I was thinking about coming back tomorrow night, maybe a little earlier," she said. "Would you be able to make it?"

Davis wanted to say yes, but, instead, for several reasons, he said, "Afraid I can't tomorrow night."

She leaned into him, and there was a gentle comfort in her weight. "What about night after tomorrow?"

A dozen thoughts waltzed through Davis' brain. Easy to figure out what he should say. But he didn't say those words. What he said was, "No guarantees, but I might be able to."

She lifted her face to his and Davis made another poor choice.

All the way home, Davis felt as guilty as if he'd done a whole lot more than kiss a pretty woman. He was damn grateful Ellen was asleep when he finally crawled into bed. For what seemed like a small eternity, Davis lay on his back on his side of the bed, staring out the window at the stars and an uncertain moon, watching the movement of the maple leaves, thinking about what he'd done, and what he needed to do. Before he reached any decisions, the waves in his brain began to smooth out and Davis let sleep take him.

Fourteen

Headlights stabbed at the darkness as the Chevy eased off the highway. Gravel crunched beneath the tires and a rabbit bounded out of the shafts of light into the darkness. The car eased to a stop in front of a small frame house, half-hidden in a stand of scraggly locusts, cedar, and sumac.

In daylight, the house was revealed as little more than a shanty, a one-bedroom dwelling, built before the Great Depression for a sharecropper or the hired help. Nice enough when new, now long abandoned, leaning south, paint peeling and blistered, floorboards rotting, it was barely habitable, fit more for field mice and sparrows than humans. Yet, on the swaybacked porch, a man rocked slowly in a one-armed wooden rocking chair left behind decades ago by the last man who'd tried to make an honest living on the place.

The driver sat behind the wheel for a moment, took a final drag off her cigarette, popped the door open, and flipped the cigarette into the night. She watched the red end pinwheel into the blackness, took a deep breath, and picked her way through the shadows to the porch.

A single lamp burned inside the shack and what little light that passed through the single window and open door was rapidly consumed by the night. A thin shaft of yellow fell across the face of the man in the rocker, so that the woman could make out the slant of his right cheekbone and the curve of his jaw. Boards creaked beneath her as she stepped onto the porch.

"He find you?"

"Yes." She paused, took a step closer to the rocking man. "Lawton, he seems like a nice enough guy. You sure you want to go through with this?"

Lawton Turner leaned forward and spat into a decrepit lilac bush. "Damn it all, Tanya, I've told you plenty of times that he is the son-of-a-bitch who got me run out of Pratt County, and the prick personally responsible for me losing better than two years of my life stuck in a lousy, stinking prison cell. So, like I told you, I aim to see that the bastard pays."

Tanya leaned against the wall of the shack, thinking about what she wanted to say. No way in hell did she want to cross Lawton Turner at any time, certainly not when he was riled. She tried to put a smile in her voice, the way her mother had taught her. "Honey, sure I understand and I'd want to do the same, only this Davis Wells guy doesn't strike me as an easy target."

"Damn, woman, did I ever say it was going to be easy? No, I said I was going to make him pay, and, by God, I am. I am going to make that asshole pay, professionally and personally. So don't try and stop me, or you just might get your tits caught in the meat grinder."

She could hear the anger running through his voice like a live electrical current, and she eased back a step. She knew she needed to calm him down, and she knew silence wouldn't do it. It never had in the past, at any rate. Her brain was whirling, trying to come up with a few good words to say. She peered up at the sky, focusing for a few seconds on the cool, shining stars. Then she turned and stepped closer, gently pressed one hand against his left shoulder.

"I understand, baby, and I'm sure not going to mess anything up. Only that I don't want you to get hurt."

She could feel his muscles bunching up under the thin shirt he was wearing, and for a heartbeat she thought he was going to explode. Then she felt the muscles begin to relax, and she sighed as the tension began to drift from her body as he wrapped his arms around her and pulled her against him. He didn't lift weights, or work out, but she could feel the strength rippling through his muscles. There were times when she relished that strength, and times when she feared it so much she wanted to cry and run away.

"Don't you worry about nothing, honey. It's like my old man always said, 'a man needs to pay his debts.' And I owe Davis Wells one helluva a debt, which I aim to pay back real soon, with interest. Now, you'll be fine if you just do what I tell you, when I tell you, and if I tell you."

He pressed his thin lips against the crown of her head. "You got that, baby?"

"Sure, Lawton, I've got it. I understand, and you can count on me. You know that."

"Good. Now go and get those clothes off and crawl between those sheets. I'm going to smoke me a joint and then I'll join you." He kissed the corners of her mouth. "We've got a little business to tend to ourselves."

He turned her around and swatted her on the butt. "Go on, now, and get yourself ready for some good lovin'." He laughed a little, and she smiled and stepped in through the open door, moving quickly, yet softly, so as not to upset his sudden good humor. The sheriff, she thought, would just have to look out for himself. Like she'd told Lawton, he seemed like a nice man, but a woman had to take care of herself first, and crossing Lawton Turner was one move she never intended to make.

Fifteen

Fireflies flickered in the yard. The moon had climbed into the crown of the maple, and creamy clouds drifted on a dark wind. All the lights were off in the house and when Davis turned his eyes south, he could see the glow of Kansas City.

They had come out after supper, strolling together through the dusk, carrying a pair of folding chairs they'd placed at the edge of what had been the garden when Davis' dad had lived there. For better than sixty years, he'd raised a garden, and now that plot of ground he had so carefully tended was going back to what it had been before man, at least the white man, arrived. Davis could never make up his mind if that was good or bad.

They'd talked for a while, not about anything in particular, drifting instead from one subject to another—it didn't much matter what they talked about as long as the conversation wasn't about anything important.

By the time the dusk had died, she'd grown silent. They hadn't argued, so Davis didn't figure her for mad. Maybe tired, or sleepy, or maybe she had drifted off again—off to that place where he wasn't allowed. Davis was considering going inside and getting a beer when his cell phone rang. He dug it out of the left front pocket of his jeans and answered without noting the number.

"Hey, boss, you got a minute?"

"Sure, Willie. What's up?"

"You know Birdman, right?

"Who?"

"Birdman Williams. One of my informants. He's the guy that gave us the tip that broke the Miller case."

A vision began to emerge from the mist inside Davis' brain. "That skinny-assed doper who lives in the trailer park behind SafeCo?"

"That's him."

"Okay, so what's new with Birdman?"

"Well, I'd been out patrolling and rolled back to the station about twenty minutes ago to wrap up my paperwork before the shift ended. So, when I get out of my cruiser, I hear something over behind that scraggly tree at the corner of the station house. I wander over in that direction, not knowing what in the hell to expect, and all of a sudden this guy steps out."

"You had your weapon drawn, I hope."

"Sure thing, boss. It's a badass world out there."

"Good. Now what happened?"

"Right. So I had my weapon out, and the safety off, and my finger on the trigger when the guy speaks. Says, 'Don't you recognize me, Hensley?'"

"Well, it took me a minute, but then I did. So I said, 'Well, if it ain't Birdman Williams.'" Then I asked him what the hell was he doing hiding behind that tree like he was aiming to ambush me. And right then he gives me the come-here finger-wave and we stroll on over to the real deep shadows out by the dumpster. Once we get there, he tells me right off. Well, first he asks me for a cigarette."

"All right, all right, I don't need to see the movie. Just tell me what he said."

"Okay. What he said was that he wanted to talk to you."

"To me? Now why in the hell would Birdman Williams want to talk to me? You're the man who knows him."

"Can't rightly say on that, boss. But I can tell you what he said."

Davis tried to keep the irritation out of his voice, but Hensley was damn sure going the long way around the barn tonight. Davis made himself take a deep breath, held it for a five count, then let it out.

"So tell me."

"Okay. What he said was that he wants to meet you tonight."

"Me? Why does he want to meet me? You're the cop he knows and he was already talking to you."

"Can't say, Davis. Just that he wants to talk, and only to you. Figured he must have something really important to tell you."

Davis couldn't begin to imagine what Birdman Williams knew that was so important that he would only tell him. Davis couldn't see where he fit in this picture.

"Said he wants to meet you tonight."

"Willie, it's late. Tell him tomorrow night."

"Can't. He's gone already."

"Damn."

"Hear ya, boss, but he said he had to see you tonight 'cause he was leaving town again in the morning."

"Didn't even know he'd been gone."

"Yeah, he's been over to Warrensburg for the last six months. Went down there to sponge off his sister and got picked up drunk as a skunk, trying to boost a couple dozen cartons of smokes. Judge gave him a year in the county jail, but he got out early 'cause they ran out beds and needed his for a guy accused of murder."

"Okay, okay. When and where does he want to meet?"

"You know the old Lion Uniform plant, right?"

"I know it."

"Good. He said to meet him behind there in an hour. Behind the building, there are three or four old picnic tables rotting away. Birdman said to meet him at the farthest one from the loading dock. Said to come alone, and no tricks."

Davis couldn't imagine what kind of tricks the Birdman thought he might try to pull, but he only said, "Thanks, Willie. I'll handle it."

Then he disconnected and told Ellen he had to go meet an informant in town. If she heard him, she didn't let on. Davis folded his chair and hauled it back to the house. Like always, he never understood why a woman did or didn't do anything.

Sixteen

Behind the old Lion Uniform plant, the light was chancy. The concrete block building blocked all light from the street and the moon was half hidden by a line of trees at the end of the parking lot. The pavement was cracked and crumbling in a hundred places. Davis moved slowly, placing his feet carefully. A twisted ankle he didn't need.

He'd left the flashlight in the car. Birdman had sounded nervous and Davis didn't want to spook him. Better for Birdman to find him than for him to go Birdman hunting in the dark.

He stopped to listen, but the wind had come up since he'd left the farm and all he could hear were the leaves rustling in the tree canopy and the squeaking of a rusty hanging sign on an abandoned grocery next door.

Davis could smell water though, strong, stagnant, the scent drifting on the wind along with those of dust, motor oil, and rotting flesh. As he stood silently in the parking lot, the moon swung out above the trees and he started moving again, heading for the four picnic tables slouching under the trees. One had collapsed into a pile of boards that looked like a good place for snakes. Davis worked his way around it

47

and found what appeared to be the sturdiest picnic table. He perched on an edge, facing the trees.

He strained to hear footsteps, but the only sound was the whispering of the leaves as the wind blew through them. As he slowly swung his head around in a half-circle, Davis tried to think what Birdman might have to tell him. He didn't have a clue.

After a few minutes, he quit thinking about Birdman and started thinking about Ellen. She'd been more quiet than usual lately and Davis wondered if the cancer had returned. If it had, that was really bad news. He didn't think she could handle much more, not after what she'd been through. He felt bad, not being able to make her feel better, and maybe a little guilty, too. Still, he was no doctor. Anyway, he was entitled to a life, too. Of course, he remembered all those in sickness and in health words, but every human had limits. At least that's what he told himself.

Clouds drifted across the face of the old man-in-the-moon and the darkness closed in, thick, heavy, full of mysteries. Davis peered into the blackness, but all he could see were shadows shifting with the wind. If Birdman were out there, he was lying low.

Davis glanced at the luminous dial of his watch and decided to give Birdman twenty more minutes. Then he'd call it a night. That would give him plenty of time to make a quick stop at Missouri Wet. He wondered if Tanya would be there. Only he wasn't sure if he wanted her to be there.

Davis started counting seconds in his head. When he reached one hundred, he pushed off the picnic table and started drifting toward the trees.

Halfway to the tree line, a bird whirled up out of the darkness, nearly crashing into him. Seconds later, Davis caught the bird's silhouette moving rapidly skyward. Another sound, fainter, yet distinct, drifted to him and he came to an abrupt halt, his right hand gripping the butt of his revolver.

Before he could act, a voice called from the deep shadows of the tree line, "That you, Sheriff?"

"It's me. That you, Birdman?"

An arm stretched out of the darkness, motioned him closer. Davis started walking, listening intently as he moved. Maybe it was the darkness, or the wind, but the whole setup felt like a trap. Birdman didn't worry him much, but the tension in Birdman's voice put his nerves on edge.

Davis stepped inside the greater darkness and leaned against a tree trunk. A faint rustling sound carried above the wind. Birdman's scent drifted on the wind. The man needed a bath.

A hand rose up out of the darkness and pressed against Davis' left shoulder. Then it slid down his arm, as though verifying he was real.

"Sheriff?"

"It's me."

"Thanks for coming. Was scared you wouldn't make it tonight."

"You in a hurry, Birdman."

"Yeah, I got to get out of town first thing in the morning."

"Bus doesn't leave till ten o'clock. And that's if it's on time."

"I know. Only I'm not taking the bus. Got a friend going to carry me to Independence. We're leaving when he gets off work."

"When's that?"

"He gets off at four o'clock. Works over to the Purina Plant in Kansas City. Then he's got to drive home. But we'll be gone afore first light. We got to be. Just got to be."

"What's your rush? Kill somebody?"

Feet shuffled in the dead leaves trapped in the ankle high grass. "Naw, I ain't killed nobody. You know me, Sheriff, I'm not a violent man. Heck, I've never even owned a gun, much less used one." That was a lie, but truth was an elusive creature for Birdman.

"Then why do you have leave?"

"That's why I wanted to see you, boss."

His ramblings made no sense. Davis was tempted to turn around and head back to his vehicle. But Birdman's fear was palpable, thick enough to cut with a knife.

"I'm here, so tell me what you need to."

Birdman leaned in so close Davis could smell the foulness of the informant's breath. "You 'member Lawton Turner?"

"Sure," Davis said. Who could forget that badass? He'd killed both Pike brothers over a drug deal gone south, and burnt down the houses of half-dozen other dealers, simply because his mind tended that way, before Davis and three of his officers had trapped Turner in the old Lewis place late one afternoon. Maybe trapped wasn't the right word as he'd damn near shot his way out after dark, blasting Deke Wilson in the leg and shooting the hat off Davis' head. Now that he thought about those days, it came to him that it had been Birdman's tip to Willie that had allowed them to find Lawton Turner in the first place.

"Well, he's back," Birdman whispered, turning his head toward the street as he spoke.

"What? He's supposed to be in state prison somewhere out west. Wyoming, maybe, or Utah."

"Yeah, he was. Only it was Idaho, and word is they voted in some liberal prison reform and he got out New Year's Day. Either that or he escaped. He's a slippery bastard, you know?"

"Yeah, I know. But how do you know he's here? Is that fact, or just rumor?"

Birdman poked Davis' chest with a bony finger. "Seen him with my own eyes coming out of his folks' house just afore dark day before yesterday. Might have seen him one other time, but I couldn't swear to that one."

It had finally occurred to Birdman who the two people were he'd seen that morning he'd come to all alone in the middle of nowhere. He didn't figure the sheriff would be happy knowing one of his informants was passed out so close to his house.

Davis felt his guts start to churn. "Sure you saw him?"

"With my own eyes."

"Yeah, but how straight were you?"

"Man, I was an arrow. Ain't had nothing for almost three days now and my guts are eating me alive."

Either Birdman was telling the truth or he was on his way to Hollywood, Davis decided. He asked the question that had been bothering him since Willie had told him about Birdman's call. "How come you're still here?"

Birdman sighed. "Onliest reason I'm still here is I couldn't get a ride out until tomorrow. You know Turner has to be looking for me. Might have put a price on my head, too. Only I figure he wants to off me hisself." Birdman sighed again, then touched Davis' right shoulder.

"I'd better slide now, Sheriff. I know he's out there somewhere toting a bullet with my name on it."

"Want me to lock you up, Birdman? I could have you transported to Independence or even Kansas City. He couldn't get at you then."

A stray shaft of moonlight fell on the two men then and Davis could see Birdman's gaunt, bony face. The informant grinned as he shook his head. "Thanks, boss, but I purely can't stand being cooped up. Besides, Lawton Turner has an in with a lot of guards and deputies. Maybe not yours, but a lot. If I was locked up anywhere close, he'd find me."

"How can you be sure?"

Birdman showed Davis the teeth he had left. "Do the math, man. You know how piss-poor guards and deputies are paid, and Turner's got more money, or at least access to it, than the whole town of West View. Thanks anyway, but I'm better off on my own."

Davis started to say something, but Birdman cut him off. "Now, don't worry. I've still got a few friends and a good place to go to ground. Old Birdman will make it, Sheriff. Always have, always will."

For a moment, Davis thought the man aimed to keep talking, but if he had, he changed his mind, clamping his mouth shut and giving Davis a light punch on the arm.

Judging by his looks, Davis figured it was close race between crack and Lawton Turner over which killed him. He knew he was aiding and abetting a druggie, but Davis dug a twenty out of the left front pocket of his pants and palmed it to the Birdman.

The little man grinned, murmuring "Thanks, man," as he turned. Davis watched Birdman work his way deeper into the shadows. He listened until he could hear only the wind in the treetops. The sheriff counted to sixty, whirled on his heel and started stepping for his vehicle.

Seventeen

In the deep, shifting shadows beneath the trees there was safety, at least the illusion of being out of harm's way. Birdman leaned against a tree trunk and tried to think what he needed to do next. Of course, what he really needed to do was to get the hell out of town. But that would have to wait for morning. Having a little money felt good, unusual, but definitely good. Birdman had lived hand-to-mouth for so long he couldn't really remember any other way.

His stomach growled as he tried to recall his last good meal. He knew he should probably stroll on out to the bypass and hit one of the fast-food joints. He was too nasty to go into a sit-down place, even if it was only a Denny's. Yes, he should wander out and get him a good meal, but he knew he wouldn't.

He could always bum food off Deke or Jason, or hit the men's shelter. No, twenty bucks would help him ease through one more night. And that was all he needed, wanted. At least for now. Sure, he knew he needed to get straight, but getting straight was not easy. In fact, it was hard, hard as hell. The hardest thing he'd ever try to do.

In the welcoming blackness, Birdman grinned at his foolish self. Hell, once he took the first toke in his early teens, he'd been off the path and he'd never gotten straight, not for more than a few days, anyway. Maybe someday he would. Maybe. Yeah, maybe.

But someday was a long way distant down a dark and winding trail, and his brain was too nervous, bouncing around like a damn pinball, and he couldn't think straight till he got out of town, out of the reach of Lawton Turner, out of the Grim Reaper's path.

His mind, well what was left of it, made up, Birdman took a deep breath, expressed the air from his lungs and started walking like his ass was on fire. He wasn't far from Delbert Griffin's place, and Delbert always had merchandise. Birdman had one Andy Jackson in his hot little hands and promise glimmered in the darkness like the campfires of the dead.

Eighteen

Willie Hensley and Tommy Smith were both in the main office when Davis walked in the next morning. Willie stuck up a hand.

"Let me grab a cup of coffee and then let's go to my office."

"Sounds good. Meet you there."

Davis poured a cup and smiled at Claudia.

She made a face. "Mayor Gregory wants you to give him a call. First thing, he said."

"Give him a call back and tell him I'm in a special meeting on the Chisholm case," Davis said as he walked by. As he closed the door to his office, Tommy yawned and Davis remembered the deputy had just finished his shift.

"Thanks, fellas. Hope this won't take too long. Expect at least one of you is probably ready for some breakfast."

Tommy was leaning against a filing cabinet. He smiled, stretched, and said, "No hurry."

The sheriff maneuvered around to the business side of his desk, eased the cup of coffee down, and sat in the old wooden swivel chair that had been there long before he took office. A construction crew was pounding away on the building across the alley that ran behind the office. It had been vacant for years, but Davis could remember when the owners had sold suits, shirts, and ties for men.

Change. Change was always there. Change was the only certainty in the world. You didn't have to pay your taxes, although going to jail was often the result, and death was really only the ultimate change. His life was changing for sure. Change had been coming on for months, since before Ellen got sick, maybe for years. He had sensed it coming in his bones. Sensed it the way he could feel a storm blowing in long before the first dark cloud smeared the horizon. As he sipped his coffee, Davis thought about what the next change might be.

Tommy yawned again, loudly, and Davis shook off his daydreaming and came back to the gray-walled room with the photograph of old Harry S on the wall beside a calendar from two years before he had kept because he liked the photo that accompanied September. The photo was a long-lens shot of Monument Valley. For as long as he could remember, he had liked the flat land and the sand and the sagebrush, with the red rocks rising up like missiles ready to launch at a baked enamel sky.

"Wish you were out there, boss?"

"Sometimes, Willie, sometimes."

The city garbage truck rumbled by and he waited until it passed before he got down to business. "Saw Birdman last night."

Willie sat up straighter. "So you two did hook up. He have anything interesting to say?"

Davis lifted his coffee cup off the desk and eyed his deputies through the steam. "Actually, he did."

Tommy rubbed a forefinger through the dust atop Davis' desk. "Well, you gonna tell us?"

"Right now." Davis sipped at the coffee, then set the cup back down on the desk. "According to the Birdman, Lawton Turner is back in town."

Willie snorted. "What's Birdman smoking these days?"

"Claimed he saw him with his own eyes."

"His vision isn't always twenty-twenty. But he has passed on a couple of good tips over the years. Including, if I remember right, one that led us to Lawton before."

Tommy leaned forward. "You believe him, Sheriff?"

"Hard to say for sure, but if I had to bet, I'd put a few dollars on yes. Birdman was scared last night. So scared I could smell the fear. Thought a couple of times he was going to piss his pants."

"All right," Willie said, "let's talk about Lawton. Why would he come back to Pratt County where he's well known? He had to know he couldn't hide out here for long before somebody recognized him."

Tommy shifted in his chair. "He could hole up somewhere."

"Nah," Willie said, "you don't know Lawton. That's one man who has to have action. One of those who's always looking for action, or trouble, or both."

"But there's no real action in Pratt County."

"Something's brought him back." Willie rubbed the back of his neck with the palm of his left hand. "Question is, what is it?"

"Maybe he just wanted some home cooking."

"Tommy, you're a real funny guy. Now let's get serious."

"Okay, Sheriff."

"Davis will do when we're behind closed doors." He took another sip. The coffee was still too hot to enjoy. Willie looked like he had something to say. Davis leaned back. "What's on your mind?"

"Was wondering how long Lawton had been back."

"Don't know. Birdman didn't say. Where you headed with that thought?"

"Okay, you know we've had an uptick in ODs the past few weeks and Lawton was heavy into trafficking. Just trying to put two and two together."

"That's a thought. Why don't you look into that? And Tommy, you give the folks out at the state prison in Idaho a call and get them to email us the most recent photo they have of Turner. Then get copies printed off and pass them around town. Plus, slip a copy to everyone who is snitching for you and the others. Tell them to be sure and call if they see anybody who even faintly resembles the man in the photo. Tell them just to call, and not to try and do anything else. Not even follow him. Unless he's had a Road-to-Damascus experience, for sure Lawton Turner is one violent son-of-a-bitch."

They both stood and started for the door, but a pair of stray thoughts had sprung up in a dark corner of his mind and Davis wanted to try them out.

"Now remember, he's got family in Pratt County, including his mom and dad, if they're still alive. Wonder if he has any brothers or sisters? Cousins, even, or uncles, aunts?"

Willie made a face. "Seems like maybe he had a brother, but I couldn't swear to it."

"No clue," Tommy said. "He was gone from here before I started."

"No worries. I'll get Claudia to do some research." Davis rubbed at his face.

"You know, fellas, one thing that keeps circling in my mind is just how truly terrified Birdman was last night. I don't think he was ordinary scared, or was paranoid on account of some drugs. I think the man really was afraid for his life."

Davis took another sip and swallowed. "It was like he'd seen Lawton commit a horribly violent act and was afraid he was going to be the next victim. Now, I don't know anything. All I'm saying is to keep your eyes and ears open and don't go down any dark alleys alone until we get this joker back behind bars."

"You think he'd hurt a police officer?"

"Don't know, Tommy, but if he's come home to seek retribution, then the Pratt County Sheriff's Office is sure as shit going to be number one on his list. After all, we're the ones who had him trapped at the old Lewis place."

"Never did see how he got out of that house."

"Me either, Willie, but he did. Keep in mind that he's one slippery bastard. Be sure and tell the other deputies about him." Davis pushed himself up out of the swivel chair and picked up his coffee cup. "I've got some business to tend to."

"Going to see the mayor, boss?"

"Nope. Going to interview Mark Chisholm's girlfriend. Don't forget, we've got an OD to get to the bottom of."

Nineteen

"So you and Mark were friends?"

"Yes, we went all the way through school together. We've been friends a long time."

The girl wasn't looking at him. She was staring out the bay window in the living room of her house. A sugar maple grew a few yards outside the room and Davis could see the leaves ruffling in the wind and a patch of blue sky beyond. He didn't have a clue what the girl was seeing. Her body was in the room, but most of her mind was elsewhere. She hadn't even noticed she used present tense when talking about her friendship with Mark. Her name was Karen Ross and she had light brown hair and a smooth, soft-looking face. She was pretty, in a nice, old-fashioned way.

"Understand you and Mark dated some."

She gnawed at her lower lip. "Actually, we dated quite a lot."

"Then you were like boyfriend-girlfriend?"

For a moment she didn't answer. Davis could hear people moving around the house, a rattle of pans in the kitchen, faint notes of a song he didn't know from a radio he couldn't see. Her father had greeted him when he first arrived and he'd caught a glimpse of a woman he guessed was Karen's mother standing in the next room. They'd both retreated, leaving him alone in the living room with the girl. He'd been told Karen had a brother, but he hadn't seen him and wasn't planning to.

A quick movement of her head brought him back to the moment. Her damp eyes flitted across his face, then drifted to a painting hanging on the wall above a piano. The painting was a copy of an El Greco. Davis wondered who the art lover was in the family.

"What do all these questions have to do with Mark?"

"We're trying to find out who might have sold or given Mark the drugs that killed him. I'm trying to get a better picture of him. Often knowing more about the victim—who he hung out with, what places he frequented—can help put us on the path to solving the crime. I know these questions are difficult for you, but I figure you want to help us find out the truth. Right?"

She sniffed as she turned her face toward the window again. The aroma of meat and onions frying drifted into the room and Davis heard his stomach grumble. He hadn't eaten breakfast and old man time was closing in on noon. Thinking of noon made him think of Gary Cooper. *High Noon* was just about Davis' favorite movie, but he wasn't Marshall Will Kane; he was the sheriff of Pratt County, saddled with an investigation going nowhere fast and a life that was sliding downhill like a sled on ice.

"Karen, were you and Mark boyfriend-girlfriend?"

She studied her hands. "I guess so."

"So, spending all that time together, you guys probably talked a lot. You probably got to know him pretty good."

"I guess so.

"What did you guys talk about?"

She sighed and he couldn't miss the exasperation in that sigh.

"The usual, I suppose."

"Movies? Weather? Sports? What your friends were up to?"

"Yeah."

"But being boyfriend-girlfriend, you must have talked some about more, let's say, personal matters. Like what you guys wanted to do in the future, your dreams..."

She turned then and looked at him hard, maybe for the first time. Tears shimmered in her eyes and her chin was quivering.

"Why are you tormenting me? Why? Mark's dead and all your stupid questions aren't going to bring him back. Why won't you just leave me alone?"

Davis felt like a clump of manure on the bottom of a boot, but he still needed to ask questions, questions that hurt. He was sorry he had to do it, but he didn't have a choice.

"Don't you want to know who gave him the heroin that killed him?"

She sobbed and dabbed at her eyes with a tissue. "What good would that do? All the answers in the world won't bring Mark back."

Davis glanced down at the carpet, then back at her face. "Did Mark do drugs?"

"No."

"Never?"

"No."

"Did he know people who did?"

"How should I know? Mark had a lot of friends. I didn't know all of them, not really. Not some of his baseball friends, and not some of the fans who were always talking to him, wanting to know if he'd signed a contract, that sort of thing."

She bit her lip again, then let out another sigh. "There are a lot of drugs around these days. A lot of people use drugs. He might have known some people who used drugs. Only maybe he didn't know they did, see? And I'll tell you this much, Sheriff, he never used drugs around me. The most we ever did was drink a beer or maybe have a shot of bourbon at a nice restaurant down in Kansas City. No drugs ever. Mark cared too much about staying in shape for that."

She fixed her eyes on Davis'. The tears had gone and something harder had settled in their place.

"All right, I've answered your questions. I've answered all the questions I'm going to answer. Now leave me alone. Please."

His gut was telling him that just maybe Karen knew more than she was letting on. But he could tell that more questions weren't going to get him anywhere. At least not this morning. Davis thanked her, and gave her his business card. Then he let himself out the front door and started for his truck.

He had barely slid behind the wheel when a man came hustling around the side of the Ross house. As the guy trotted up to the vehicle, Davis could see his face bore a notable resemblance to Karen's. Davis cranked the engine and powered the window down.

"Can I help you, sir?"

The man shook his head. Now that he was closer, Davis could see the guy wasn't quite a man yet, but he was more than a boy. The guy leaned closer. "Maybe it's the other way round."

"What do you mean, sir?"

The guy smiled as he stuck out his hand. Davis shook it.

"I'm Joe Ross, Karen's brother."

"Nice to meet you."

"Same here." He sucked in a deep breath and angled his face away.

"You were saying?"

He let out the air he'd been holding and swung his face square to Davis'. "I was in the kitchen while you were asking Karen all those questions."

"And?"

"And I heard you asking about Mark's friends and Karen talking about those people who liked him because he was good at baseball. Just as you were leaving, I remembered something." He made a face and paused. Davis fingered the steering wheel and waited. Down the block a car horn blared.

"It may not amount to anything, but..."

"Go on. Don't worry about what you remembered being important or not. Better to tell something that doesn't have any bearing on a case than not tell something that turns out to be vitally important."

"Well, like I said, it may be nothing, but one day I did see Mark driving around with some other girl besides Karen."

"When was this?"

"Couple of weeks ago."

"You know the girl?"

The kid shook his head. "Don't believe so. See, I was sitting at a red light and barely got a glimpse as they drove by, so I can't give you a good description. But it looked like the woman had a thin sort of face and I'm certain she had real dark hair. That's what caught my eye, really. Karen has light brown hair, you know, almost a dark blond. And this woman's hair was much darker, black maybe, at least very dark brown."

"And I'm guessing Karen never colors her hair, right?"

"Right. I see her every day and know for sure she doesn't color her hair. Doesn't even put those streaks in her hair like some other girls do. Oh, what do they call them?"

"Highlights?"

"Yeah, highlights, that's it. Karen never even highlights her hair."

"And you're sure it was Mark Chisholm you saw?"

"I'm sure, Sheriff. See, I've known Mark all his life. Played ball with him and double dated with him and Karen, gone to at least a dozen Royals games with him. Yeah, I recognized him, all right. Knew him like a brother."

A robin hopped across the driveway in front of the truck and the boy's eyes followed the bird. Then they swung back to Davis.

"Well, that's it, Sheriff. Told you it wasn't much. Just something I thought I'd better tell you." He glanced over his shoulder at the house. "Expect I'd better get back in. Lunch should be ready. Hamburgers, baked beans, and potato chips. Sorta like a picnic, huh?"

"Thanks, Joe. Really appreciate you sharing this with me. You never know, it might turn out to be important," Davis said, although he doubted it would amount to anything more than Mark Chisholm seeing another girl on the side. Then he remembered the boy had said woman and not girl.

"Quick question before you go, Joe. One time, you said the person in the car with Mark was a girl, but another time you used the word woman. Which one was it?"

Karen's brother squinted his eyes and twisted up his face as he thought. Davis' stomach grumbled again.

"At first, I thought it was a girl. On account of Mark being younger than I am, see. But there was something about her face that made me think of somebody older. Older looking, anyway. But, like I said, I only caught a quick look."

"Thanks."

"Sure," the kid said. Then he turned and jogged back the way he came. The robin rose before him, winging for the cloudless sky.

Twenty

Davis washed the last of the pots and angled it on the drying rack. Then he tugged off his plastic gloves, grabbed a cold beer from the fridge, and strolled outside.

Daylight, which had still held while they had been eating supper, was in full retreat now. Only a thin mauve line outlined the western horizon. The air had fallen still and lightning bugs flashed their secret code. Davis strolled across the side yard toward the old garden. Ellen was sitting there, a few feet from the remains of the garden. In the starlight, he could see the back of her head. Before supper, he'd hauled out a pair of lawn chairs and she was sitting in one. He eased down in the other.

"Nice night, isn't it?"

Without turning her head, she said "Very."

"Good day? Bad day?"

"Pretty good, I suppose. Dr. Felling called today."

Phone calls from doctors always made Davis nervous. He never knew whether they were going to bring good news, or bad. Lately, the news had been more bad than good. He sipped at his beer. "What'd he have to say?"

"He said the blood work I had done last week came back better than he had hoped."

Now, what the hell did that mean? He decided to try for positive. "That sounds like good news."

For a minute, she didn't respond and he wondered if he'd missed something. Then she made a small sound in her throat. "The numbers were better than the last time. He thinks maybe we've got it in remission."

"Well, that's wonderful. Best news we've had in quite a while." He leaned over and kissed her cheek. "Aren't you happy to hear that?"

"I guess so, but Davis, remission isn't usually permanent."

"I know, I know, but let's just take it for good news and enjoy that. What do you say?"

"Okay," she said. The word sounded wistful to him, but then at times his imagination was a touch vivid.

Roughly fifty yards beyond the far end of the old garden plot, now going back to nature, there had once been a pond that both his father and grandfather had used to water stock. When he was a kid, his dad had stocked it with bluegill and catfish. Before he'd gone off to college, they'd spent many a late afternoon and evening fishing there together. Those outings had been fun—just sitting by the water, talking, watching the clouds move across the sky and their bobbers go up and down, and later, after Davis got to be eighteen, maybe drinking a beer or two. They hadn't caught a lot of fish, certainly never a big one, but then that had never been the point.

After Davis went off to college, his dad had taken sick and couldn't keep the pond dredged and cleaned out. Gradually the cattails, moss, and algae had taken over. These days the old pond was nothing more than a damp patch of ground. All the fish were gone, but a few frogs still hung on in the dampness and he could hear them cranking up now. Their night calls gave him an idea.

"Wanna take a walk down to the old pond?"

She looked at him then, with starlight painting her face so that he could see her eyes searching his face. Davis didn't know what she saw there, but she smiled and rose easily. He pushed out of his chair and

65

they began to stroll alongside the old garden. At first, they moved out of step, but gradually their strides began to match and they strolled smoothly past the ancient asparagus bed, and the remnants of the potato hills and corn rows, then started down the slope toward what remained of the pond. The moon was above the trees and moonlight flowed before them like a river of fragile silver. Here and there, Davis could still make out patches of the old path, and off to the west, he could see the roof of the old Groves' place.

A whippoorwill started up between the pond and the road and Davis could smell honeysuckle in darkness. Ellen stumbled against him and when he held her for a moment, he could feel the bones pressing against her clothing and wondered, not for the first time, how she kept going. As they resumed walking, he recalled that one of his Uncle George's sayings, and he'd had a gracious plenty of them, was that there was a damn good reason men didn't give birth. Thinking of Uncle George made him smile. But Uncle George had been dead for ten years, and his dad and mom were dead, along with lots of other good folks, and the worst of it was there wasn't a damn thing Davis could do about that.

"You okay?"

"I'm fine, just took a bad step."

Several responses flickered through his mind, but he didn't voice any of them. Instead, he slowed and draped an arm over her shoulders. They walked the rest of the way in companionable silence.

The frogs were going strong and there must have been a thousand fireflies flickering on and off. Pratt County had been in a dry spell, but Davis could smell the dampness that was all that remained of the pond and feel the softness of the ground beneath his feet. Ellen's face was splashed with moonlight. She looked thin, in an unhealthy way. The years had settled on her harder than she deserved. But lately it had seemed to him that nobody got what they really deserved. For damn sure, he knew he hadn't.

Davis figured that telling other people how to act wasn't his call to make. Since high school, he'd realized that trying to live other people's lives for them was one of his biggest faults. So he kept his mouth shut, settling for holding her close as he listened to the night tuning up.

After a moment, she stirred. "Davis?"

"What?"

"You think things will ever get back to some semblance of normal?"

Now, he wasn't sure what Ellen's definition of normal was, but Davis had an idea where she was headed, so he said "Sure. Why I bet this time next year we'll look back on these times and smile."

He couldn't tell if she believed him, or if she knew he was lying. What he was sure of was that she had settled more tightly against his chest. He hoped she was going to have a good night, but, after a moment, he heard her sob, Seconds later, crying wracked her body.

Davis held her and stroked her hair. He felt sure there were words he should have been saying, but he couldn't think of them. Words were one thing he'd never been good at. So he held her and stared out over the top of her head into the darkness. Something soft and warm touched his left hand and then he felt her right hand stroke his left cheek.

"Davis, I'm sorry. So sorry for being sick all the time. I know I'm not a good wife for you right now, but I'm trying, honey, I really am."

Right then, remembering some of his less than loving thoughts, he surely felt small. Davis swore silently that he'd change, but deep down he knew that was only remorse talking. Over the years, he'd made thousands of promises to himself. Most had been the kind that were easy to forget, especially in the daytime.

He loved Ellen all right, it wasn't that. It wasn't that at all. He understood life wasn't always fair, but he also knew there were times a man needed more than promises, more than memories, more than the emotion of love. At least he did. Davis knew what he was thinking wasn't right and he was fighting it like hell. But it had been over a year with nothing more than boney hugs and passionless kisses.

In an effort to clear his mind, Davis took a deep breath. Thinking along those lines was nothing more than going down a dead-end road, he knew. He was only fantasizing, he told himself. That was all. Simply pure fantasy. He couldn't, wouldn't treat Ellen that way. Not and live easy with himself, he couldn't.

Slowly, sounds of the night came drifting back. Davis could hear the frogs and, in the distance, cattle settling down for the night. Nearby, an unseen creature rustled through the tall grass. Davis looked up at the sky, and thousands of stars and the man-in-the-moon looked back at him.

Ellen coughed and he peered down at her. Tiredness lined her face.

"Ready to go back?"

"But a kiss first, okay?"

"Sure," he said and bent and pressed his lips softly to hers. She was so fragile he was afraid of hurting her.

Without either of them speaking again, they started back, holding hands—just like when they had been in high school. Davis thought about how she had been then, so gorgeous and vivacious and sweet it made his heart ache. And now, and now, and now what? Oh hell, life was just too damn sad sometimes. Too sad for words.

Moonlight painted a path before them, and he squeezed her hand and thought about how lucky he was to have her at all. Davis knew he'd never been any sort of a prize; he'd truly never understood why she'd ever even gone out with him, let alone married him.

All the way back he remembered those days, wishing, at the same time, that they would come again. But he felt certain they never would. And that made him so damn mad he wanted to bust the world right in the mouth.

But he merely walked Ellen back to the house, then helped her upstairs and into bed. He wanted to stay for a few minutes, hold her and tell her how much he cared for her. But she was tired, so tired he knew he needed to go so she could get some sleep. He'd always felt sleep helped almost any situation. He went back downstairs and out the back porch door, crossed under the grape arbor and stood on top of his little mountain—the mound of dirt and grass that covered the old root cellar—where he stared out across the night, hurting inside, wondering how it was all going to end.

Out beyond the Groves' place, out toward Kansas, on a dusty side road, somebody was driving. Heading home, he figured. Davis watched the two headlights piercing the darkness, wondering where the driver was going, envying whoever was behind the wheel. He watched the headlights until they were absorbed by the great, mysterious darkness that covered everyone, saint and sinner alike.

Twenty-one

"I'm sorry to have you ask you all these questions, Mr. Chisholm."

Mark's father took off his glasses and rubbed the lenses on his shirt. Then he put them back on and stared at Davis without blinking. Somehow, wearing the glasses made him look younger.

"That's all right. Know you have to do your job."

"Yeah, I do, even though I wish I were almost anywhere else." Davis glanced out the window, then turned back to Mr. Chisholm. "You know I was fond of Mark. He was a good kid and a good athlete, and it's a damn shame about what happened."

Chisholm inclined his head and rearranged his mouth as though he were going to say something, but thought better of it and simply lowered his head.

For a minute, then two, they sat in silence. Davis didn't know how long they would have remained like that, but the phone rang twice before he heard a woman answer it. For a moment longer the two men sat quietly, listening to the faint noises from the street, mingling with the muffled sounds of a woman talking somewhere deeper in the house.

Chisholm broke the spell. "Go ahead, Sheriff, ask your questions." His voice had hardened during the silence. Davis set his jaw and took a deep breath.

"If I remember correctly, you and Mark got along pretty well."

"Mark got along with everybody, but, yes, we were close."

"Closer than most fathers and sons?"

"I'd say so."

"Then you talked a good bit?"

"More like we talked some. You know how busy young people are. His mother and I weren't seeing as much of Mark as we used to. But I suspect that's probably normal these days. What with cars and cell phones and laptops, kids branch out on their own a lot sooner than we did. A lot sooner than I did, anyway."

Davis figured Chisholm was right, but he couldn't think of an appropriate comment, so he asked another question.

"When you guys talked, did he talk about anything in particular, anything that was bothering him?"

"Mark never seemed to have any serious problems. Oh, we might talk about being short of money, or a bad grade on a test. Nothing more than that."

"Notice any changes in Mark over the past few months?"

"Not really. Mark was always a good kid. Never gave his mother or me any trouble."

"Did he drink?"

"You mean like alcohol?"

"Yes."

"Not really. Oh, I'm sure he had a beer or two, almost every kid does. Hell, I had a few beers myself when I was his age." Mr. Chisholm lifted his eyes. "Didn't you drink a beer or two when you were his age, Sheriff?"

"More than one or two, Mr. Chisholm. Now, I'm not impugning Mark in any way. I'm simply trying to find out something, anything, that might give us a lead."

Chisholm rubbed at his face, then twisted in his chair and looked out the window, his face half averted. Davis figured the man was having trouble regaining his composure, so he kept his mouth closed. After a few moments, a heavier silence than before began to infiltrate the room. When it became more than Davis wanted to hold, he stood and wandered over to a black piano standing in the far corner of the room. The cover was folded back and the keys smiled up at him. Slowly, tentatively, he picked out "Chopsticks," which reached the limit of his musical talents.

Listening to the notes, he remembered his mother and how much she had loved music, and how long and hard she had worked to make a pianist or a singer out of him. And how she had tried to hide her disappointment when he proved unworthy of her efforts.

Chisholm's voice brought Davis back to the present, back to the room. "I know, Sheriff. And I know how much Mark thought of you. It's just that nothing makes any sense to me these days." Chisholm pushed out of his chair and walked to a bookshelf, where he straightened an offending hardback. "So go ahead and ask me whatever you need to and I'll answer as best I can."

Davis turned and sat on the piano bench. "Thanks, know it has to be really tough for you, but you never know what might help." He thought for a moment about what to ask, figuring it would be best not to start with anything too sensitive.

"Had you or your wife noticed any changes in Mark's behavior recently?"

"No. I mean nothing more than since he graduated, he stayed out later at night, maybe didn't talk quite as much as he did when he was younger. But I figured that was all part of growing up."

"How about new friends?"

Chisholm screwed up his face. "Not really. Heard him mention somebody named Mike and somebody named Dave, but I think they were a couple of his baseball buddies. If I remember right, he mentioned going to a Royals game with them."

"No new girlfriend?"

Chisholm shook his head. "Not as far as I know. Mark dated Karen Ross ever since they were sophomores in high school." He nibbled on his lower lip. "I couldn't swear to it, Sheriff, but I had a vague impression that maybe he'd been spending less time with her the last few weeks."

"Any idea why?"

"Not a clue. Like I said, that was only an impression of mine. Can't give you a single concrete example."

To make it appear he was doing something besides listening, Davis jotted the girl's name down in his pocket notebook. Of course, he'd already interviewed her, but Chisholm didn't know that.

"Now, to circle back for just a moment, you know Mark drank a few beers, but didn't do drugs."

"That's right," Chisholm's voice was clipped and his eyes had grown hard.

"Anybody else ever see Mark out drinking, or with anybody unusual?" Davis could see Chisholm's face start to darken, so he added, "I'm not implying anything, Mr. Chisholm, only trying to get a lead."

At first, Davis didn't think Chisholm was going to answer, but then the man's eyes changed and he thrust out his jaw. "Now I'm sure it doesn't mean anything, but I bumped into a friend of mine, Ed Mitchell, about a week ago and we got to talking. Just shooting the breeze, reliving old times, griping about the politicians. Know what I'm talking about?"

"Yes."

"Well, anyway, Ed did mention—just in passing, mind you—that he'd seen Mark out to a bar one night, and he was at a table with a girl Ed didn't know. Now, Ed's known Karen ever since she was a baby. He's her uncle by marriage, see, on her mother's side." Chisholm stopped then. Davis felt like the man had more he could say, but Chisholm tightened his lips and Davis decided, at least for the moment, to move along the way he'd lined out.

"Don't believe I know Mr. Mitchell, at least by name. But sounds like you know where he lives."

A faint smile formed on Chisholm's face. Davis could see where he'd be a nice fellow to know under different circumstances.

"They used to live right across the street. That yellow house there." Chisholm pointed to a frame two story shaded by a pair of maples. Two little girls were playing dolls under one of the maples, and a little fuzzy dog sprawled at their feet.

"But Mitchell got a big raise a couple of years ago. He works for UPS. Once he got that, why he and his wife moved out to that new subdivision on the south side."

"The one they built on the old Hull farm?"

"Yes. Hated to see that place developed."

"I know," Davis said. "Hulls used to have a huge tobacco allotment and the best dairy herd in this part of the state. I knew one of the Hull boys." He grimaced. "That was a long time ago, though. Can't remember his first name now."

"Was it Jason?"

"No, but that sounds close."

"Then it had to be Jordan. He was the taller Hull boy. Good basketball player."

"That's him. Wonder what ever happened to him?"

Chisholm's face rearranged itself. "He got killed over in Afghanistan a few years ago. Roadside bomb."

Chisholm sighed and looked down at his shoes. "Knew the family from church. Went to Sunday school with Jordan's dad. He was some older, but a real nice fellow. Help a man anyway he could. His boy's death took all the starch out of him, though. Always figured that was the big reason he sold out."

"Any idea where the Hull family is now? I always liked Mr. Hull."

Chisholm shook his head. "No. Bob Hull quit coming to church after Jordan's death and I didn't even know they sold the farm until I saw it in the *Chronicle*."

The two men fell silent. Davis figured Chisholm's mind was drifting back across the years. It was that sort of silence. He let it run for a couple of minutes, then said, "Mark get anything out of the ordinary phone calls or letters?"

"Not that I know of. But, like everybody else, he had a cell phone. Not like the old days. Before cell phones came along, we had only one phone and that one was in the kitchen." Chisholm mustered up a weak smile. "Easier to keep up with things that way.

"I agree," Davis said, "but if you'll let me borrow his phone, I'll have one of my deputies do some checking." He made seven meaningless dots below Ed Mitchell's name in his notebook.

"All right," Chisholm said, "I'll find it and give you a call."

"Now, Mark wasn't drinking a lot, but since he died of a heroin overdose, I have to wonder if he was doing any drugs. Experimenting maybe?"

He'd pissed Chisholm off. Could see it in the man's face. Davis watched Chisholm swallow the anger down. For a moment, it appeared it was going to choke him, but the man worked through it.

"No. I'd bet money on that. Mark was a smart kid. Knew the dangers of drugs. He'd never have even considered doing drugs."

"Probably right, Mr. Chisholm," Davis said, closing his notebook and slipping his pen back in his shirt pocket. A long time ago he'd learned that ninety-nine percent of parents didn't have a clue what their children were really doing. Sad, sure, but it was also the truth.

He stood. "Thanks for your time, Mr. Chisholm. I'd better get rolling." Davis fixed a smile on his face. "Always something to do in this business, you know."

Chisholm walked Davis to the door without speaking. He held the door for Davis and shook his hand. Davis tugged his cap down and stepped outside. Sunlight was fierce and heat radiated off the sidewalk like fire.

Twenty-two

The highway was new and smooth. It was one Davis had never driven on. Either there hadn't been much crime in this part of the county or he'd been spending too much time behind his desk. He eased along, looking for signs of the old Hull place. There weren't many, and if he hadn't been looking, he'd have missed them.

The old tobacco barn still stood on the rise, and Davis caught a quick glimpse of the remnants of what had once been considered the finest cherry orchard in Missouri. The stream with no name still meandered off into the swale where the Hull brothers had set up their campsite in those distant summers. Because he knew where to look, he could make out the foundations of the cabins that had housed the Hulls' slaves before the Civil War and catch a glimpse of the family graveyard nestled inside a circle of cedars.

But that was all.

Even the old frame homeplace had been razed. A new two-story, multi-colored brick had taken its place. The old oak that had been dying since he was a kid had been cut down and the cattle pastures, wheat fields, and tobacco patches had been replaced by houses, tennis courts, and swimming pools. As he turned in between two massive stone pillars, Davis caught sight of a section of a golf course under construction. Golf had never been his game.

Mitchell's house was a low, rambling ranch on the second street. A new Dodge truck sat in the driveway and a large concrete birdbath decorated the front yard. Davis turned into the driveway and cut the engine. Before he could pop the door, a tall man wearing glasses, accompanied by an old dog casting a distrustful eye, stepped out the front door and started ambling down the sidewalk.

"Help you?"

"I'm Davis Wells, Pratt County Sheriff, and I'm looking for Ed Mitchell."

The man twisted his mouth around and said, "I'm Ed Mitchell. What am I supposed to have done now?"

Davis let that part about now slide. "You're not in any trouble, Mr. Mitchell. I'm simply looking for some information."

The tall man's face relaxed a little then, but his eyes stayed hard. Davis wondered what the fellow was hiding.

"What sort of information?" The man worked his face into what might pass for a grin. "I'm not the sort of guy who pals around with gangsters and such."

It was Davis' turn to fake a grin. "Didn't figure you were, Mr. Mitchell." The dog had wandered over and was sniffing his shoes. Davis stretched out a hand and scratched the old boy between his ears.

"Actually, your name came up in a case I'm working on."

The worried look slid back across the man's face. "What case is that?"

"I'm looking into the death of Mark Chisholm."

"Oh, okay. Yeah, I knew Mark. Know his dad better. Fact is, we're sorta kin and we used to be neighbors. Dave's always been a good guy. Hate it real bad about Mark."

I leaned back against the vehicle. "Heard you saw Mark recently."

"Me? Nah. Oh, you mean out to that bar?"

"That's it."

A breeze had come up while they'd been talking and it had blown a swatch of hair across Mitchell's forehead. He pushed it back and stared off across his neighbor's yard. The old dog had finished smelling

Davis and he wandered over to the shade thrown by the vehicle, easing down there with a sigh.

"You want to hear about that?"

"That's why I came, Mr. Mitchell."

"Well, it was one night after work, say three, four weeks ago. Couple of the guys I work with wanted to go out for a beer after work and asked me to come along. Now, I usually come straight home, but I knew Sue had an Eastern Star meeting that night, so I went."

"Who were the guys?"

"What?"

"Who were the guys who asked you to go out for a beer?"

"Oh, why it was Joey Hemphill and Paul Bennett."

"I know Bennett." Davis wrote the two names down in his notebook.

Mitchell licked his lips and shifted his gaze back to Davis as though he wondered if the sheriff expected him to say more.

"Go on."

"Well, it didn't amount to much. We all drove separate and I had to stop on the way to gas up, so by the time I got there, they already had a table and a pitcher. Anyway, I drank a couple of mugs with them while we shot the breeze. Really, Sheriff, that's about it. Didn't stay long on account of I needed to let the dog out, 'cause Sue was at her meeting."

"But you saw Mark?"

Mitchell rubbed at his face. "Yeah, I saw him, right enough. Surprised the hell out of me, too, 'cause I never figured him for that kind of a place. Him being younger, see, and such a good ballplayer."

"You couldn't be mistaken, Mr. Mitchell?"

Mitchell shook his head and smiled. "No sir, Sheriff, I've known, er knew him, since he was a little boy barely out of diapers. For sure it was him."

"And he was drinking?"

"A bottle of beer was sitting on the table in front of him, but I didn't see him drink any. 'Course I wasn't there long and the joint was crowded that night. Only happened to notice him when I went to take a leak."

"But you're sure it was him?"

"Sure, for certain."

"Was he alone?"

"Nope. He was with someone."

"Man or woman?"

"Woman."

"Describe her to me."

Mitchell squinched up his eyes and curled his mouth as though his lips were in pain. The sunlight was hot and Davis could feel sweat starting to roll under his uniform. Off to the south, somebody was running a tractor.

"Now, it's always kinda dark in there, right? And, like I said, it's been a few weeks, but as I remember she had dark hair."

"Black or brown?"

"Hmm. Couldn't swear to it, but I'd say black." Mitchell rubbed the back of his neck like he was a tired man. Davis figured what he was tired of was questions.

"How old would you say she was?"

"Oh gosh, I'm no good at guessing women's ages, especially when I never got a real good look, but I'd say thirty, give or take."

"Was she thin, or heavy?"

"Hard to say for sure since I never saw her standing, but I remember thinking her face looked thin." Mitchell quit rubbing his neck and folded his arms. He cocked his head and stared straight into Davis' eyes. "Now don't laugh, Sheriff," he said. "But if you want the way I'd describe her, well I'd say she was pretty enough, slightly dark complexioned, thin, like I said, and hungry looking. Yes, sir, I say that woman sure enough had a hungry look about her."

Davis thanked the man and climbed back in his vehicle. All the way to town, Davis studied on what Mitchell had called that hungry look. Davis thought about the time he'd seen it. Then he wondered if he'd ever see it again.

Twenty-three

Davis wheeled his vehicle into the driveway, stopped, and got out to check the mail. The sun was a bloody smear at the very edge of the western sky, but the heat was still stifling. Before he could get back in the vehicle, sweat had formed on his forehead and upper lip and begun to pool on his chest. Davis climbed back behind the wheel and sorted through the mail. Deep down, he knew he was also killing time. Some days he found it tough to see Ellen, the way the cancer had taken her.

The mail didn't amount to much: a bill from the electric company, one of Ellen's home decorating magazines, a letter from his congressman Davis didn't bother to open, a letter for Ellen from her sister, and a flyer that promised the reader the vacation of his or her life—at $3,750 a ticket. One picture on the flyer showed a train climbing one of the mountains in the Rockies. That would be all right, but not at such a price. Davis tossed all the mail onto the passenger seat and shifted into drive.

Ellen was sitting in a lawn chair under the grape arbor. Shadows lay thick there, but the heat was hanging on. He peered over her shoulder, looking west. Not a cloud in the sky. Back in March, they'd had seven straight days of rain. Now, the last rain he could remember had been a brief hard shower just after dark ten days ago. It had been ninety every day since, and not many degrees cooler at night. He swiped at the sweat soaking his face as he gazed down at his wife.

Her face was deep in the shadows, but a random strand of light from the kitchen fingerpainted a single stripe down her right cheek and glittered in her eyes, and for a moment it was easy to imagine her young and healthy, the way she'd been when they'd married. Those wedding day promises suddenly weighed heavy on his shoulders. Davis bent and kissed her forehead. Then he laid the mail in her lap.

"You got a letter from Linda."

"Oh, good. It's been a while since she's written." In the bluing light, he could see her smile. "I bet she'll give us an update on the boys. They're both in high school now, you know."

"That's right," Davis said, although he wasn't thinking about their nephews. He was thinking about another boy—the one it hurt so bad to think of, the one they never talked about—and he wondered where he was and how he was doing. But that was a path that led only to pain and he surely didn't any more of that right now, so he crossed the porch, picked up another lawn chair, and set it down beside her. As he eased into the chair, he caught a whiff of her perfume and the memories flowed fast and sweet.

"How was your day?" she asked.

"All right. Couple of interviews on the Chisholm case, plus the usual paperwork." Davis reached over and rubbed the back of her left hand. "How was yours?"

She turned then so that he could see her teeth, white in the gathering darkness. "Not so bad. I worked almost all of the crossword puzzle, talked to Mary Ann Fenster for half an hour, ate the last of the minestrone for lunch, and took a nap."

"Sounds good. You hear from the hospital?"

"No, but, Davis, I think I might feel a little stronger this evening. That's good, isn't it?"

"Sure it is," he said, wondering whether she really felt stronger, or was only trying to put up a front.

He didn't push it, though. Maybe she did feel stronger, or maybe she only wanted so strongly to feel better that she'd managed to convince herself. For sure, Davis didn't know. After all, no person ever really got to know another one—not down to their core, to their essence—did they? And everybody told lies. Little ones to protect someone else's feelings, momentous ones to protect themselves, and all sorts of lies in between. Way he saw it, the lie she might have just told was a small one, a lie that hurt no one, except perhaps herself. So he let it stand; perhaps it would purchase her a few precious moments of peace.

He didn't say anything more and neither did she. They simply sat in silence, watching the light fade out of the day, listening to the sounds of the night coming alive, thinking their own thoughts, dreaming their own dreams.

When the stars began to come out, he felt her left hand slip into his right one and Davis squeezed it softly and wondered where they went from here. A car passed, rolling west, and he watched the headlights push into the darkness, wishing he were in his vehicle rolling west, heading toward Kansas. Only that was just another of those lies, one he told himself with great regularity.

When Davis could no longer see the headlights, he squeezed his wife's hand once more and gently disengaged, stood, and walked into the kitchen. She hadn't cooked, so he made a sandwich, which he ate standing at the sink, watching fireflies flickering on in the yard and trying to make sense of the Chisholm case, and his life, asking once more why the cancer had hurt the woman he loved.

After he ate, Davis wandered down the hall and took a shower. He toweled off, slipped on his robe and climbed the stairs to their bedroom. The lights were off, but he could hear her breathing softly. He hesitated, then tossed his robe on her dressing chair, crossed the floor, and slid between the sheets as naked as the day he was born.

She didn't say anything and Davis wondered if she'd fallen asleep. But in a moment, he felt her turn to him. She rested her head on his chest and he wrapped an arm around her shoulders, holding her close while they waited for sleep to rescue them from their demons.

Twenty-four

Thompson Road broke off Highway 57 just beyond the old Perkins' Grocery, bent east, then continued for almost a mile before coming to a sudden dead end at a barbed wire fence that marked the western boundary of the Pete Anderson place. Over the years, people driving down there, whether by accident or on purpose, had carved out a rudimentary turnaround. Two large oaks had grown up at the apex of the arc of the turnaround and this night a truck was parked beneath them. The truck was turned so it faced down Thompson toward the highway. Under the oaks, the air was one shade short of black. The truck's headlights were off and the only light came from the intermittent glow of the cigarette of the man behind the wheel.

The truck had been in the same position since dusk had started falling and the man had scarcely moved, changing position only enough to twice pull a cigarette out of the pack in his shirt pocket, then light and smoke it, and once to turn his head and spit out the window. His eyes were narrow slits in face, searching the darkness for light.

Just before ten o'clock, an owl whirled its way out of the darkness and settled on one of the branches that overhung the turnaround. Seconds later, as though the bird's movement had been some sort of a signal, headlights pierced the darkness.

Behind the wheel of the truck, the man took a final drag off his cigarette, flipped it out the open window and sat up straighter, his eyes opening wide, watching the oncoming headlights.

A car came down Thompson Road, rolling slowly, rocking in the dips, swerving a few degrees now and then as the driver maneuvered to avoid the deeper potholes. The owl perched statue-still on the limb, eyeing both vehicles.

The driver of the car swung around a final pothole and eased his vehicle to a stop. For a moment, he thought about turning his motor off, decided against it, took a deep breath, and opened the door.

He got out slowly, a touch stiff after the long, slow ride, took a careful look around, then walked slowly but steadily toward the truck.

The driver of the truck shifted position behind the wheel, but made no move to get out. Wrapping the fingers on his left hand around the wheel, he ran his right hand through his hair. His eyes stayed fixed on the man approaching his truck.

Five feet away from the truck, the walking man halted, peered through the darkness, and cleared his throat.

"That you, Lawton?"

"Yep, Brooks, it's me. Who the hell else would it be?"

Oblivious to the darkness, the man shrugged. "You never know. Didn't want to take any chances."

"No problem. You got the money?"

The man patted his shirt. "Right here. You got the stuff?"

"Sure enough. Let's see the cash."

The man hesitated, then realizing that just standing there in the dark trying to see through the blackness wasn't a winning hand, reached inside his shirt and pulled out an envelope. He paused, took a step closer as he extended the envelope. Seconds later, he felt it disappear.

When the man in the truck remained silent, the other man felt his insides start twisting around on themselves as a thin sheen of sweat broke out across his forehead.

Inside the truck, the man flicked on a small flashlight, then thumbed through the contents of the envelope. Satisfied, he stuffed the money down the left front pocket of his jeans, picked up the flat box on the seat beside him and thrust it out the window.

He didn't let go, however, even when the other man's right hand closed on one end of the box.

"You know Davis Wells, Brooks?"

"Sheriff, ain't he?" The other man shifted his weight, conscious of his heart beating, wondering where the conversation was headed.

"Yes."

"Yeah, I know him. Not well, but I know him. Why?"

"Don't worry about why, just tell me if any of his people, or his friends, are your customers."

The other man rubbed at the face with his free hand. "Why do you want to know that?"

"That's none of your damn business. Just tell me if any of your buyers are kin to Wells, or a friend of his."

"Hard to say, but maybe. I'd guess a couple of the boys who played ball for him back when he coached American Legion probably know him pretty good. And maybe Peggy Carmichael. She works down at City Hall. Think she dated one of his deputies for a while. What the hell you want to know that for, Lawton?"

"Never you mind, Brooks. You tend to your business and I'll tend to mine. Now, which deputy did she date?"

"If I'm remembering right, she dated that Smith boy for a few months last year. Remember seeing them and the sheriff eating lunch together one day, and I know she used to traipse over to the sheriff's office some. Saw her coming and going more than once. But I don't see where any of that signifies."

"Thinking never was your strong suit, Brooks. Now, you just make sure the Carmichael babe and those ball players get a little extra of the special stuff in that box real soon. You hear me?"

The man standing in the darkness was confused. None of the conversation this night made any sense, but he had no desire to hack off Lawton Turner. He'd seen what happened to men, and women, who had. So, he simply said, "I hear you."

"All right, then. And Brooks..."

"Yeah?"

"See that you contact those folks real soon. Tell them you've got some really good shit." For the first time, the man behind the wheel inclined his head out the window. "Like the next day or two. I'll be watching, see, and I'll know. And I can promise you one thing, dog, you don't want to mess with me on this this. Understand?"

Brooks Hampton's right leg trembled slightly and he could feel his palms starting to sweat. He needed to piss off Lawton Turner like he needed another hole in his head. That image chilled him to the bone and he swallowed hard and said, "I understand."

Lawton Turner released his grip on the box then, started the truck, and shifted into gear. He flipped on the headlights and inclined his head further out the window.

"Give me ten minutes before you drive out. No use arousing suspicion. And don't forget what I told you. That would be one damn bad mistake."

Before Brooks Hampton could get out a coherent response, Lawton Turner's truck was rolling...tires spinning, dust rising, headlights probing deep into the overarching night. The owl sat silently on his limb.

Twenty-five

Davis was on his third cup of coffee and second batch of expense reports when the phone rang.

"Sheriff Wells speaking."

"This is Martin Phillips, Chief of Police at Independence."

"Hey, Martin." Davis knew the man slightly from a couple of law enforcement conventions. "What's up?"

"Well, Davis, I think we've got your boy over here."

Davis' heart started pounding and he made himself take a deep breath. It couldn't be, he told himself, it just couldn't be. "What are talking about, Martin?"

"Ever hear tell of a fellow called Birdman?"

Davis felt his nerves ease off. "Might have," he said, wondering as he did what he would have done if the police chief had said another name.

"Well, my boys found him just after daylight yesterday morning. One of them thought he recognized him, but it was real hard to tell."

"What do you mean, hard to tell?"

"Well, Davis, when a man's had his face beaten so badly that both his eyes are almost swollen shut and a bunch of his teeth have been knocked out, it makes it right hard to make a positive identification."

Davis felt his heart slowing. Sure, he hated it for Birdman, but at least it wasn't the person he'd been thinking of, the one whose permanent loss he wasn't sure he could take.

"What makes you think he's my boy?"

"'Cause when he finally came around, first thing he did was say your name. Figured that put him a whole lot more in your ballpark than mine."

Davis hated to ask. More trouble he didn't need, and Birdman struck him as nothing but trouble. "What did he want?"

"Your old buddy, Birdman, wants you to come get him. Now, ain't that friendly?" Chief Phillips laughed and Davis decided not to speak to him at the next convention.

"Can't you just put him on a bus or have one of your guys drive him over? I've got an officer on vacation this week, so I'm a man short. We'll reimburse you for the bus ticket or the gas."

"Sorry, Sheriff, but I'm down two officers myself and another one called in sick. Besides, your buddy said he wouldn't talk to anybody but you, so don't send one of your deputies."

Davis looked at his coffee, then out the window. A fistful of clouds rode low on the horizon, but they weren't big and they weren't dark and the time and temperature sign on the Bank of Weston said it was already seventy-nine degrees and not quite ten o'clock. He thought about Ellen for a moment, and then he thought maybe he ought to treat himself to a drink after work.

"You still there, Davis?"

"Yeah, Martin, I'm still here. Now, where is Birdman?"

"He's at CenterPoint."

"The hospital?"

"Told you somebody beat the living hell right out of him."

"I've never known the Birdman to have the price of admission to the movies, let alone a hospital."

"Nowadays, hospitals have got to take anyone, especially if they show up at the emergency room, which is where my deputies took Birdman. Millionaire or bum, doesn't matter. You show up at the emergency room for treatment, they got to take you. But now that they've patched your boy up and given him something for pain, they're ready to cut him loose."

Davis thought about that for a minute. Probably there was some smart remark he could make, but he seemed to be fresh out of them.

"Oh, and I'd bring someone with me. Birdman isn't exactly mobile at the moment. He needs, shall we say, a little extra support to get around. Plus, he's scared so damn bad that there must be something out there that's pretty damn nasty. Might not hurt to have backup.

"I'm rolling in five."

"You're welcome, Davis," the man said and laughed again. Davis cradled the receiver and signed the last of the forms in the folder he'd been working on. Then he pushed away from the desk and walked out into the reception area. Claudia was at her desk and Willie was checking his cell phone.

Davis smiled at Claudia. "I'll be out a while. Got to roll over to Independence and pick up one Birdman. Doubt I'll be back till mid-afternoon, if then."

Willie looked up from whatever text he was reading. "The Birdman? Our Birdman?"

"Actually, he's more yours than ours, but yeah, it's the same guy."

"Why in the hell is Birdman calling us? What does he think we are, some sort of taxi service?"

"You busy?"

"Nothing that can't wait."

"Come on then. Ride with me and I'll tell you all about it."

~ * ~

Traffic was light heading east on I-70 and Davis drifted into the fast lane and pushed up to eighty-eight, then held her there. When he squinted his eyes, it almost felt like he was flying. He enjoyed the sensation of leaving his problems behind and, for a couple of heartbeats, thought about not stopping at Independence, but rolling on as far as a tank of gas would take him, and then getting out and starting walking, going as far as his legs would carry him. But Davis knew he was only daydreaming and daydreams never came true, not any more than the nightdreams did.

Willie's voice brought him back to reality. "So somebody beat up old Birdman?"

"That's what Chief Phillips said."

"Wonder who did it?"

"Guess we'll find out soon enough," Davis said as he flicked the blinker and began easing right. The exit for CenterPoint was only a quarter mile away and a notion about who might have beaten Birdman was starting to grow somewhere in the bowels of his brain. Willie pulled out his cell phone and Davis pressed on the brake pedal.

Twenty-six

"My name is Davis Wells and I'm the Pratt County Sheriff." Davis pointed a finger at Willie. "And this is Deputy Hensley. He's here to assist me. Chief Phillips phoned me this morning and asked me to pick up a patient of yours."

The woman behind the emergency room desk wiped her nose with a tissue as she squinted up at Davis. "What's the patient's name?"

Now came the feeling foolish moment. He'd been dreading it, but couldn't figure out any solution except to come straight out with the truth. "Afraid all Chief Phillips told me was that his nickname is Birdman."

The receptionist's eyes grew wide, then her mouth twisted around on itself and she said, "You mean the man who was beaten?"

Willie leaned in. "If he's a skinny fella with bad teeth and long greasy hair, then that's who we're looking for."

The receptionist sniffed like she'd gotten a good whiff of skunk spray or the town dump, and puckered up her mouth like she was trying to eat lemons straight. "The man you want is in the next room on the right, third bed from the door." She paused, her eyes flicking from Davis to Willie, then back to Davis. "Don't suppose you gentlemen are going to pay the patient's bill?"

Davis shook his head, gave Willie the eye, and started walking. He heard the woman sniff again, then sigh. Everybody's got troubles, sister, he thought. But he kept his mouth shut and stepped down the hall.

Martin Phillips hadn't been lying. Davis would have hated to have to officially identify Birdman. Both his eyes were still swollen almost shut, his lips were puffy, and his nose was out of align. Davis had seen people walk away from head-on car crashes and not look as bad. Abrasions and bruises spotted his face and Davis wondered what the rest of Birdman's body looked like, but not enough to check it out.

Birdman was lying on a gurney, a sheet pulled up to his chin. Willie walked around the gurney and eased a hand on Birdman's left shoulder. "Birdman, how you doing?"

Birdman sniffed and mumbled "Not so hot."

"What the hell happened, man?"

Birdman raised himself up on one elbow, groaning as he did, and looked around. A nurse with flabby arms walked by and Birdman waited until she'd passed. "Not here, fellas, too many people, if you know what I mean."

Willie patted Birdman on the shoulder and Davis saw their source wince. "Can you walk, man? Or do we need a wheelchair?"

"I'll get a wheelchair," Davis said as he turned, headed for the hallway. He'd had enough of hospital rooms during Ellen's stays. The sooner they got out of CenterPoint, the better he'd feel.

Davis walked down a long corridor that ended in a T. He chose right at random and went down another corridor that ended in another T. A guy was coming from the left pushing an extra-large trash can on wheels. Davis waited for him and caught his eye.

"Help you, Officer?"

"Looking for a wheelchair. I've got to get a witness to my vehicle." Well, for sure Birdman had witnessed something. Whether he would tell any of it was another story.

The man with the can had a funny look on his face, and Davis wondered if the guy believed him. But, after a moment, the man said, "You wait right here and I'll bring you one."

"All right," Davis said and leaned against the wall. The man pushed his cart down a short corridor, moving more quickly, and turned right. When he was out of sight, Davis pulled out his cell phone to check for messages. No service, so he closed his eyes and thought about Ellen, and then about the woman with the dark hair he'd met the other night, and finally about crossing over to Kansas. He was still thinking about Kansas when he heard a rumble coming his way. He opened his eyes and watched the man push a wheelchair toward him.

The man stopped and made an odd little flourishing gesture with his right hand. "Here you go, sir."

It was then Davis noticed three of the man's fingers on his left hand were missing. "Thank you."

"You're most welcome," the man said as he smiled.

His teeth didn't look much better than Birdman's, and Davis wondered what the guy's story was. Everyone had them, of course. Stories, that is.

Davis considered offering the man a dollar, but the guy had already turned and started back the way he'd just come, so Davis decided to leave well enough alone—something he didn't always do—and started pushing the wheelchair Birdman's way. As he moved down the corridor, memories of pushing Ellen in and out of hospitals rose up and he worked to swallow them down. Doctors and nurses hurried by him in both directions; every one of them looked like they knew where they were going with their life and Davis felt the envy rising.

Twenty-seven

"It was him, all right."

Davis glanced in the rearview mirror. Birdman was leaning his head against the passenger window and his legs were sprawled across the seat. Davis wondered if the dummy had unbuckled, but decided not to make an issue of that. The little man had enough problems.

Willie turned his head and said, "Who you talking about, Birdman?"

"The one what did this to me."

"Well, who was it?"

"Just who I warned you about, Sheriff."

"Lawton Turner? Lawton Turner did that to you? 'Cause if he did, all you'll need to do is agree to testify, and we'll take photos and have you examined. Then, I'll get the county attorney to issue me a warrant and we'll arrest Turner, put him right back in prison."

"That's right," Willie said. "For sure, he's violated his probation with an assault and battery charge. What do you say, Birdman, was it Lawton?"

"Will you swear to it?" Davis added.

Birdman sat up then, ramrod straight. If the man had been standing, Davis would have described him as at attention. "Hell, no,

I ain't testifying to nothing, and I ain't swearing out no warrant. Not against nobody, and for damn sure not against Lawton Turner."

Birdman twisted around and pressed his battered face against the glass. Davis looked over at Willie and shook his head. For the next four or five minutes, they rolled in silence. Finally, Birdman swung his head around and caught Davis' eye in the rearview mirror.

"This beatin' I took is mostly your fault, Sheriff, though I know you never intended for it to happen."

Davis shifted his eyes back to the road, wondering what Birdman was driving at. "And how is Lawton Turner beating the living hell out of you my fault?"

"Now, I ain't never said Lawton Turner touched me and don't go saying I said that. 'Course now, he might have kicked me some in the ribs."

"Well then, who in the hell beat you up?"

"He had some men. Must have been three or four of them. They took turns, see?"

"Yeah, I see, but how does that make it my fault?"

Birdman rubbed his nose and turned his head to stare out the window. "Lawton said he had nothing personal against me. All he wanted from me was to deliver a message to you. As for the beating, that was simply to make sure I remembered the message."

Davis could feel his throat tightening. He swallowed and said, "What was the message?"

Birdman licked his bruised lips and cleared his throat. He was looking everywhere but at the mirror. Davis began to get the urge to pound on Birdman some himself. "Come on, give?"

"Now don't get mad, Sheriff, but Lawton said for me to tell you personally that he's going to hurt you worse than you ever hurt him."

Willie twisted around in his seat and stared at Birdman. "And what the hell is that supposed to mean? Hurt worse? Hell, Lawton never was hurt, at least not by anybody on the force. Fact is, he wasn't even really roughed up."

"Damn, Willie, I don't know. Don't get so riled up at me. I'm only delivering the message."

"Yeah, well that's a damn cryptic message. You sure he didn't say anything else?"

"Not really, only said the sheriff had better watch his back, cause he was a comin' for him when he least expected it."

Davis was suddenly aware his hands hurt from gripping the steering wheel so hard. He loosened his grip and tried to wrap his mind around Lawton's message. All he'd done was enforce the law and helped put a criminal in jail. As far as Davis knew, he'd never broken any law, other than speeding and maybe littering. So how was Lawton going to make it worse on him? Nothing about the message made sense and he wondered if Birdman had smoked a few too many brain cells over the years.

They were well north of Kansas City and, barring trouble, they'd be home in ten minutes. Davis checked the mirror again. Birdman had his eyes closed and Davis couldn't tell if the man was asleep or faking. "Want me to drop you off at your mom's? Or at one of your friend's?"

"No way, man. Lawton knows all my hiding holes. Loan me enough money for a bus ride out of town, boss, and you'll never hear from old Birdman again. I swear."

Willie snorted. "We've heard that one from you before. You're going to have to come up with a new line, Birdman."

"But I really need to get out of town. Lawton's liable to kill me next time. I'll go to Denver, or Phoenix, or Portland—it don't matter. But I've purely got to get out of this state. Missouri ain't big enough for both me and Lawton Turner."

He groaned and hugged his abdomen and Davis figured Birdman wasn't in good enough shape to do much traveling, even if the county or city had been willing to spring for a bus ticket. He glanced at Willie. "Any ideas on where we can stash him?"

"Hmm, nothing pops to mind, but let me think on it. If I was a single man, I'd stick him in the basement for a couple of weeks and let him heal up. But with Delores and the kiddos, well, that won't work."

"No," Davis agreed. "Nothing comes to mind for me, either. Everybody I've thought of has a wife and kids, or parents, or they'd be too scared to take him on."

Birdman groaned and sagged in on himself. Davis wheeled the vehicle through the curve where McCuller's Dishbarn had stood for twenty years before it had burned last fall and then up Beecher's Hill and by Weston High before he turned into the back parking lot of the station. Birdman was snoring and the other two men got out of the car and left him sleeping. Davis halfway hoped Birdman would be gone when he came back out.

Twenty-eight

Davis spent the rest of the afternoon working with Claudia on a breakdown of Pratt County crime statistics for Judge Gorton. As they walked out the door, late afternoon sunlight slanted directly into their faces and they stood blinking like drunken owls. Then Davis pulled the bill of his cap down, wished her a pleasant evening, and started walking for his vehicle, glancing around for Birdman. He didn't see the man and felt tension draining off him like sweat. He opened the door and let the heat roll out in waves. His line of vision shifted, toward Kansas, but all he could see was the back of the *Chronicle* building. Davis counted to thirty and started to climb in. One hand was on the steering wheel when he heard footsteps.

"Sheriff?"

Davis turned to the voice. It had come from the deep shadows between the city building and the Mexican restaurant that had gone in what had been Winslow's Shoes when Davis was growing up. He'd eaten there a time or two and they grilled a tasty tilapia, but still, he missed the shoe store. But then he was getting old, and memories had a way of deceiving.

"You alone?"

Davis took a look around. "Seem to be."

Birdman eased out from the shadows, turning his narrow head left and right like he was expecting a Sioux war party to ambush him at any minute. Then he hobbled to the vehicle and, grunting some, climbed in the passenger side. That wasn't what Davis had planned, but he didn't say anything, only swung on board and started the engine.

Davis punched the air-conditioning to max cool and powered the windows down. "Where to?"

"You tell me, boss. Been trying to think of someplace safe all afternoon and all I got was a headache." Birdman groaned and let his head fall back on the headrest.

"What about the men's shelter? You could at least grab a shower and they usually have extra clothes lying around."

Birdman jerked like he'd been tagged with a cattle prod. "Man, I can't be staying in no shelter. Way too many men in there, men who never learned to keep their mouths shut. No sir, I need to get out of this town. Make that out of this county. Matter of fact, I need to get out of state, like way out of state. California say, or maybe Arizona. Some place warmer, see, on account of the winters here are so damn cold." He sniffled and shifted in his seat, pressing his face closer to the open window. He was shaking, too. Only Davis didn't know if that was from fear or from needing a fix.

"Say, Sheriff, you have any luck with that bus ticket?"

"Nope. Budget's tight this year. Besides, the county has put you on a bus twice before and you keep showing back up."

"Yeah, but you know what they say—third time's the charm."

"Good try, Birdman, but no go." Davis powered the windows up and shifted into gear. At the end of the street, he turned left and they rolled west. At the light, he hung another left. Two blocks later, he eased into an alley with no name that ran between the Pratt County Men's Shelter and an empty building, which a few months before had housed an Allstate insurance agency. Davis pulled into the gravel parking lot behind the shelter, shifted into park, and turned to look at his passenger. Birdman had a sick look on his face and a trembling in his jaw.

"Tell you what, Birdman, I've got to run by KFC and pick up supper for me and my wife. Now, you go on in there, grab a quick shower, and find some clean clothes. I'll swing back by and we'll figure something out. What do you say?"

He should have just brushed off the bum back at the office, or dumped him at the shelter, but Davis supposed he felt sorry for the man, and maybe he was recalling a bit of the Christian charity the Methodists used to go on about when he was a kid and went to Sunday school and church now and then. Or maybe he was playing a bank shot with Old Man Karma. Anyway, he'd made his play and he'd see where it took him.

Birdman was still studying on the situation, so Davis gave him a nudge. "What do you say, Birdman? It's fish or cut bait."

Birdman sighed deeply, like something awful was paining him. "Can you bring me back a two-piece box?"

"All right," Davis said. He could do that much for a witness, although he still wasn't sure exactly what the man had witnessed. "Now, hop on out."

Birdman sighed again, but popped the door and eased out. He trudged across the gravel like he was headed for a prisoner-of-war camp. Davis shifted back into drive and headed for the Colonel's.

Twenty-nine

"Care if I eat now?"

Davis glanced at Birdman as he shifted into gear and the truck started rolling. "Only if you're careful and don't get greasy chicken everywhere. I got plenty of extra napkins, so use them. And don't throw any bones out the window. As sheriff, I can't condone such behavior, or be seen driving around a druggie throwing chicken bones out of a moving vehicle. You got me?"

"Got you, Sheriff," Birdman mumbled around a mouth full of the Colonel's original. "I'll be careful."

Davis grunted, simply to let Birdman know he was still paying attention and turned the vehicle toward home.

Birdman finally came up for air when they were about a mile from the farm. "Sorry about that. Guess I was near to starving." He dabbed the seat with a napkin. "Hope I didn't make too big a mess."

"Don't know about a mess, but you surely ate like a dang starving dog. How long since you ate last?"

"Good question. Only I can't rightfully tell. Guess you could say my mind's been elsewhere."

They crested the ridge by what folks still called the Tyler Bundle place and Davis shot a quick look across the wheat field that sloped down to a willow thicket fronting an old pond that still held water. A memory of swimming in that pond with the Bundle boys, Tommy and Lucas, flashed across his mind. Tommy was dead almost twenty years now. Drunk driver had killed him coming home from Drayton one night. Davis hadn't seen or heard from Lucas since the funeral. Billy Hickman had told him that he'd heard Lucas was working for the National Park Service somewhere out west, but Billy wasn't what you'd call a reliable source. Funny, Davis thought, how life shifts things around on a man. He'd known those two boys all through school and after, and now one of them was long dead and other was long gone. As for himself, well he'd have to say the jury was still out.

They were down the slope then, going by Blake Mitchell's feed lot, with the D. C. Groves farm coming up on the left. He slid a glance over at his passenger. Between the shower, clean clothes, and some food, the man was looking better. Bruises still marked his face and neck, but the purple was beginning to yellow around the edges, plus his eyes were open wider than they had been.

"Birdman," Davis said, "now that you've got your belly full and your mind back, pray tell, what the hell are we going to do with you?"

Birdman tilted his head like a bird, squinched up one eye. "Was still kinda hoping for that bus ticket to Bakersfield."

"Well, sorry for you, Buckaroo, but that ain't in the cards. Don't you have any friends or family who would put you up?"

"That's not the point, man. Sure, they's plenty that would put me up, but that don't keep me safe. Hell, Lawton could find me at any of them places and that'd just be the end of old Birdman, the pure living end, especially now that half the population of Pratt County has seen me riding around with you in your truck."

Davis hit the blinker and turned in at the gate. He braked to a stop and shifted into park. "Hold on, I'm going to check the mailbox," he said, swinging the door open and stepping into the gathering dusk.

The air had taken on a veiled bluish tinge and the breeze meandering in from the west caressed his face. The unmistakable scent of fresh mown hay rode on the breeze, mingling with other aromas: dust and sweat and something sweet blooming. Down to the south, an unseen calf called for its mother and a quail whistled from the sage grass across the road. Davis let his gaze drift across the landscape and caught a glimpse of a hawk perched on a fence post, staring unremittingly back at him. It seemed to Davis that if he closed his eyes, he would be transported back a hundred years, and, for a moment, he was tempted. But Ellen was waiting for her supper, and the Birdman was in the truck licking his fingers, too restless to stay anywhere for long, so Davis stepped lively to the mailbox and pulled the door open. It was the usual conglomeration: flyers, junk mail, a bill from one of his credit card companies, along with a letter from Ellen's aunt who lived in Sedalia.

Davis gathered them up, quick-stepped back to the truck, and tossed them on the dash. Birdman was staring out his window, looking toward the old barn in the swale. Davis shifted into drive and pressed down on the gas pedal, stirring up gravel.

He parked under the branches of the huge sweetgum that had stood in the side yard for thirty years and turned to face Birdman.

"I'm going to go in and eat some supper with the wife. Then maybe do one or two little chores. While I'm doing that, you can sit where you are, or get out and sit on the front porch, or just wander around. Stay close, whatever you do, because when I come out, we're going to take you someplace."

Davis gave Birdman his fiercest official law enforcement stare. "While I'm inside, you'd best be making up your mind. 'Cause if you don't decide, I will, and I'm just real likely to drive you back to West View and kick you out at the courthouse."

Birdman mumbled something that might have been agreement and Davis grabbed the KFC bag and the mail and headed for the house, pushing along through the gathering dusk.

The screech of the back door sounded loud in contrast to the quiet of the house. Davis paused and listened, but all he could hear was the humming of the refrigerator and the tick of the Seth Thomas that had been his grandfather's on the mantle. He wondered if Ellen was sleeping. He placed the food and mail on the table and walked out of the kitchen.

She was sitting in a rocker in the next room, which had been a parlor two generations ago, staring out the window toward his vehicle. She turned her head toward Davis and smiled. "Who's that man out there?"

Davis took a look. Sure enough, Birdman was wandering toward the old ramshackledly wooden building that, fifty years earlier, had served as a garage and workshop. "He's a witness. I've got to take him to a safe location after we eat. You hungry? I've got KFC."

She rocked slowly, her head turned again toward the window. Davis stroked her hair and wondered what she was thinking. The passage of time was marked by the Seth Thomas and a single firefly flickering in the side yard.

"Guess I could eat some."

He helped her out of the rocker and held her left hand as they walked to the kitchen. She was smiling, but it was a tired looking smile.

~ * ~

During supper she talked intermittently. Not about anything in particular, just random snatches about what she done during the day, the Navajo mystery she was reading, and a dream she'd had recently where a thousand bluebirds circled above their house. Davis half listened as he ate his chicken, thinking occasionally about what he was going to do with Birdman, the woman at the tavern, and where Lawton Turner was this evening.

After supper, he washed up the breakfast and lunch dishes, started a load of whites, and sat on the couch with Ellen while they watched a game show that was new to him. Darkness had control of the yard now and Davis knew he needed to get his ass up and tend to Birdman. He pushed off the couch.

"Well, baby, I've got to go tend to my witness. May be gone a while. Want me to tuck you in before I go?"

She lifted her face for a kiss. "No, I'm going to watch the next show and then think I'll call Mary Anderson. She called a couple of days ago wanting my recipe for spoonbread, and I promised to look it up and get back with her."

"Need me to do anything else before I go? Cup of hot tea? Candy bar?"

She shook her head. "No, Davis, I'm having a good day, and, like I told you, I'm not helpless."

"I know, but—"

"But nothing. Don't worry about me. Like I said, I've had a pretty good day. I'm just a little tired, that's all. You go on, and I'll go to bed in a little while."

He leaned in to kiss her. She smiled and gave him her cheek to peck. That was ok—ever since she'd gotten the diagnosis, he'd been squeamish about touching her. Davis recognized that made him an asshole, first class, and he told himself to straighten up, but that didn't change the way he felt. He gently squeezed her shoulders, then headed to find Birdman.

A full moon was rising and if he'd still had his young eyes, Davis would have been able to read at least the headlines in the *Kansas City Star*. Mr. Birdman wasn't sitting under the grape arbor, so Davis checked the vehicle first, then the front porch. For a moment, he stood on the front steps, letting moonlight bathe his face, wondering where his witness had wandered off to. Then he remembered seeing the man drifting toward the old garage, so he turned and started heading that way himself, dodging shadows as he followed the moonlight trail.

Birdman was there all right, sitting on a couple of sacks of grass seed Davis had bought last fall, but never gotten around to using, leaning back against the swayback wall. Davis flipped the light switch and a pair of dim bulbs flickered on. Birdman's eyes were closed, but as Davis walked across the packed dirt floor they opened.

"Hey, Sheriff."

"Birdman. How you feeling?"

"Eh, still ache right smart, but the pain's easing some and I've got a full belly, so it's all good."

"I've got some Motrin if you need them."

"Might take you up on that later."

"Just let me know."

Davis looked around at the old work bench, with his dad's tools still lying there, starting to rust, and the riding lawnmower, his son's bicycle, both tires flat, a badminton set nobody had used in fifteen years, boxes of Christmas decorations they hadn't put up last December, plastic tubs that held who knew what, three or four old Army cots his dad had bought at the Army Surplus store in Kansas City forty years ago, his fishing poles he hadn't used in ten years, and two wicker chairs of ancient vintage that Ellen usually put out on the front porch when summer arrived.

"Hope you don't mind me letting myself in. Was looking for a place to rest and the door was cracked open."

"No worries, but have you decided where you want to go?"

Birdman squinched up his face and slowly shook his head. "Sorry, man, I've been trying to think of some place safe, but not one comes to mind." He sat up straighter and looked Davis in the eyes. Even in the poor light, Birdman's bruises appeared awful.

"Did come up with one notion. Now, you'll probably say it's a crazy idea, and I'd understand completely. But I got to thinking maybe I could just stay out here. I mean on your place for a day or two, till I get my traveling strength back." He raised his hands. "Now, not your house, mind you, but say maybe I could sack out here in this little building."

Maybe because he was tired, or maybe because he was in a hurry, but Davis swallowed his first answer and thought about the Birdman's idea. He didn't like it, but he couldn't see a druggie staying long on the farm. Not unless the man could figure out a way to get high on grass seed and MiracleGro. Ever since Ellen had been unable to work at the bank due to her cancer, she'd gotten in the habit of locking things up tight at night when he wasn't home, and she knew where both his dad's old Smith & Wesson and his grandfather's .16 gauge were. They'd never had any trouble. Visitors had been limited to a handful of friends, a few stray dogs, and a dozen of Blake Mitchell's cattle getting out one time and wandering over to their front pasture. Even the Jehovah's Witnesses hadn't journeyed this far from civilization.

"I'd be real good, Sheriff. Not bother you or your wife none. You wouldn't even know I was here."

"There's no bed out here."

"Hell, I've slept in a whole lot worse places." Birdman grinned. "Now, you might not think it to look at me, but I've lived hard in my time."

Even Davis had to grin at that one. Birdman put him in mind of that old Duane Eddy song, "Forty Miles of Bad Road." He thought for another minute. "Okay, but only for a night or two. The old outhouse is still standing not far outside this building, under a walnut tree. There's toilet paper and hand sanitizer out there. I'll bring you some water before I go and we'll worry about food tomorrow. Oh, and you be damn sure and stay away from the house unless your life depends on it. You aggravate Ellen and I'll make you believe Lawton Turner is an Eagle Scout."

"You got it boss. Old Birdman will lay real low for a day or two and then I'll be on my way." He grinned like he had good sense.

Davis turned and walked back out into the night. He gathered up an old blanket he kept in the vehicle for emergencies, a couple of bottles of water from his emergency stash, and the bottle of Motrin. Wondering if he'd made the right call, he took them back to his witness.

Birdman was sitting precisely where Davis had left him, not showing any signs of planning to go anywhere soon. Davis handed him the collection, along with another of his special law enforcement stares. Birdman gave a mock salute and they parted company for the evening.

Thirty

He stood at the window, letting his eyes drift across the cleared land, out into the timber that ringed the clearing, out where the darkness was filling in the spaces between the trees and the swales, encroaching on the dirt lane that led from the highway. He knew the place—it was more cabin than house, starting to lean south, with the glass broken out of all windows but one, the porch buckling, and the roof swaybacked as an old horse.

The man remembered it as the Lucas place. Porter Lucas had been a sharecropper for Jack Deskins, who had owned the land when the man had been a boy. The man remembered this place, because Porter Lucas had fathered two sons, Paul and Stan, who the man had played with when he had been in grade school. In those days, the man had lived with his parents on the far side of the hill that rose just beyond the timber line, no more than a quarter mile from the shack. The man was Lawton Turner.

The old home place was still standing. In fact, a cousin had lived there up until last Thanksgiving, when he succumbed to a heart attack while walking his dog. Lawton would have preferred to stay there. Shadowy memories and ghosts were pretty fair company, but he figured that once Davis Wells started looking, the old home place would have been one of the first places he searched.

Lawton Turner fingered a cigarette out of the pack in his pocket, poked it between his lips, and struck a kitchen match he'd found in a dusty drawer. He drew smoke in, let it out. Still staring out the window, he said, "You understand what you're supposed to do?"

The woman opened her eyes, stretched her naked body across the rumpled blanket covering the saggy mattress, and took a long look at the back of the man she loved. At least she figured she must love him. For almost a year now, she'd lived with him, ever since he'd gotten out of prison. They'd had some tough times, sure. But they'd also had some good times. Plus, he was a strong man, a hard man, someone she could lean on. And Tanya Hurtz was sharp enough to realize she needed someone to lean on. Tanya had never considered herself to be really intelligent. However, she was honest with herself, and that honesty had helped her navigate the hard times.

"Think so."

Lawton turned from the window and ran his eyes over the woman. Whatever the sight of her slim, white body did for, or to, him wasn't apparent in his face. Prison teaches a man one hell of a lot, including how and when to control his emotions. "Let's hear it, then."

Sighing, the woman sat up, wedging her back against the brass headboard. She gave him a searching look, sighed again, then said, "I meet him tonight as planned. Let him buy me a drink, dance with him a time or two, then start leading him on. Only tonight I don't let him get very far. Sorta get his mind going in a certain direction, though." She smiled at Lawton. "Is that right, hon?"

"Close enough. Now, you be sure and encourage him plenty, only don't give too much away too soon. I want the son-of-a-bitch panting for your ass. That way, when I drop the hammer on him, the shock is going to be extra strong. And I want the prick to feel pain, the way I've felt pain these last three years. I want Davis Wells to hurt bad, hurt like hell itself had crawled up his ass and started a war."

The woman blinked, once, twice, but she didn't say anything. Barely enough light filtered into the cabin for her to make out Lawton's face. She'd seen that look before and knew what it meant. She'd also learned when to keep her mouth shut. Tanya knew she was no class valedictorian, but she was that smart.

The little room fell quiet as darkness closed its fingers around them. Although the air was still sultry, thick with the residual of the day's heat, the woman felt a chill arcing through her body. She swung her legs off the bed and began to get dressed.

"Light me one, will you, hon?" she said.

Lawton Turner grunted and seconds later tossed the pack of cigarettes to her. She caught the pack, and shook one out, stuck it between her lips. She started to ask for a match, but before she could get the words out, she noticed Lawton had turned and was staring out the window, peering out into the thickening blackness. Out in the deepening dusk, a whippoorwill started up and she watched Lawton cock his head to one side, as though he were listening intently. Whether he was listening to the bird, or to the murmurings of memories, she couldn't say. However, she did know she'd never before seen the expression that covered his face. It chilled her to her bones.

Tanya Hurtz plucked the cigarette out of her mouth and dropped it in her purse. Then she finished getting dressed without speaking. The whippoorwill sang again, and another, closer to the cabin, answered.

Thirty-one

Davis wheeled into the parking lot, parked, and sat behind the wheel until the dust and his nerves settled. Then he shut the motor off, climbed down and stood stretching, letting the day fall away. Birds chirped sleepily in the crabapple trees that bordered the east side, and the bullfrogs were starting up in the pond beyond the barbed wire behind the bar. Drifting in from the north, the breeze was cool against his face. Traffic was light and a sense of peacefulness rose in him and he thought again of the flat, lonesome plains of Kansas. Maybe he should have been a pioneer, Davis thought. And maybe he was full of shit. He smiled at his foolishness as he strolled through the cool blue evening to the bar.

Mike was tending bar and something slow and country was playing on the jukebox. Davis studied the sparse crowd without seeing one person he knew. He wandered over to the bar and sat on a corner stool with a view of the front door. When Mike finished serving a customer who put Davis in mind of an English teacher he'd suffered through at Central Missouri, he drifted down the bar.

"Evening, Sheriff."

"Evening, Mike."

"Good day in the world of law enforcement world?"

"Long day."

"What'll it be? First one's on the house."

"Thanks. I'll take Knob Creek in a tall glass."

"You got it," the bartender said and ambled away. Mike stood seven inches over six feet and must have weighed well over three hundred pounds. During his playing days at Mizzou, and later with the Lions, he'd weighed two-fifty. Bad knees had ended his pro career early.

He brought Davis' drink back and they chatted about the old days until a new customer sidled up the bar. Davis took a sip and let his eyes wander around the room. The crowd was sparse, even for a weeknight, but it was early. Lida Clawson, who been a couple of years behind Davis in school, was waitressing and he caught her eye and waved.

A couple wandered in and joined the gathering, which consisted of three or four couples, three soldiers out on the town, a half-dozen men who looked either lost or like they were primed for action, and two women sitting together. Davis wondered if they were a couple or a pair of ladies looking for love in another nowhere bar.

For the better part of an hour, Davis sat thinking about the Chisholm case, Birdman, Lawton Turner, and Ellen. He sipped his drink as he tried to make sense of what had happened. Was Mark Chisholm's death nothing more than bad luck? Or was there a batch overloaded with fentanyl making the rounds? What was Lawton Turner really doing back in Pratt County? How was Ellen truly feeling? And had he misjudged Tanya?

All that thinking gave him a headache and he wanted another drink, but knew he couldn't chance it. Being a sheriff had its disadvantages. Davis glanced at his watch. Nine-thirty had come and gone and so had ten o'clock. Time for him to head for the house and check on Ellen and Birdman. Pushing his glass away, he gathered himself to stand. Before he could move, he felt a hand settle on his shoulder. He looked up into Tanya's face.

Maybe it was nothing more than the bar lighting, but Davis seemed to see a tenseness in her face. Or maybe, he considered, he was projecting his own tenseness onto her.

She gave him a smile and said, "Well hello, stranger. Bet you were beginning to think I'd forgotten all about you. Mind if I sit down?" She gestured at the vacant stool next to him.

"Please," Davis said, knowing as he spoke the words that he should be working on the Chisholm case or tending to Ellen. Surely, he told himself, a few minutes wouldn't hurt.

As she sat down, he caught a whiff of her perfume. She smelled of lilacs.

"Haven't seen you for a couple of days," she said. "What you been up to?"

"Working, mostly. Would you like a drink?"

"Whatever you're having."

He caught Mike's eye and gave him the two sign.

"And what is it that you do that keeps you so busy you can't come and see me but once a week?"

"I'm in government."

"FBI, I'll bet." She laughed, but her eyes were busy elsewhere.

"Nope," Davis said.

Mike brought their drinks and Davis gave him a twenty. While Tanya sipped, he studied the room. The air in the bar was warm and stale, the murmurs of the crowd faint. Somebody was playing another slow country tune on the on the jukebox, but nobody was dancing. It wasn't the country he'd grown up listening to and he didn't care for it. Mike was chatting with a burly man at the far end of the bar, who Davis figured for a truck driver. A farmer, still in his overalls, ambled out of the men's room. "Slow tonight," Davis said.

"You're telling me." She laughed again as she flipped her hair, twisting on her stool. They clinked glasses and sipped. The music changed to something a bit more up tempo and Davis felt her fingers on his left arm. "Wanna dance?"

"I'm not much of a dancer. Maybe a slow one every now and then," he said. But he was only being polite. He really was a lousy dancer, but, more important, as sheriff he couldn't be seen dancing in public with a woman not his wife.

"Oh, come on, I'll bet you're a good dancer."

"You'd lose your money."

She leaned closer and fixed her eyes on his. She was so close her hair tickled his face and he could smell the bourbon on her breath. He wondered how many she'd had before she made the bar.

"Then maybe I can guess something else your good at."

Davis lifted his glass and let bourbon wet the tip of his tongue while he tried to think of something safe to say. His usual conversation gambit was the weather, but he wanted to do better than that tonight.

He leaned closer. "No, let me guess something about you."

"All right."

"Bet you're not from around here originally."

She gave Davis a funny look, before she remembered to smile. "What do you want to know that for, big boy? You gonna contact my third-grade teacher and check up on me?"

Davis tried not to show it, but he was surprised by her response. All he'd been doing was trying to make small talk. Davis wondered why such a simple question bothered the woman. Maybe she'd had a bad childhood. Hell, what did he know about women?

He laughed at her questions, then changed the subject. "What sort of work do you do?"

She rearranged her smile, then took a long sip before she answered. "I'm in sales."

"With a company I might know?"

"Probably not."

Davis could see his attempt at conversation was an unadulterated bust. He decided to adopt his mother's advice, given to him on his sixth birthday—speak when spoken to. Shifting on his stool, he let his eyes flick across the crowd again. A few more folks had drifted in, mostly singles, but a fistful of couples thrown in for seasoning. Four couples had gotten on the dance floor and they were trying to line-dance to a catchy tune he'd recently heard on the radio. Their gyrations seemed downright goofy to Davis, but then he liked a hangover better than line-dancing.

Tanya hummed to herself as she worked on her drink. Now and then her fingertips brushed against his. Davis kept his mouth shut and his eyes on the dancers. She finished her drink and went to the Ladies'. Time never stood still—Davis could feel his body growing older, seemingly by the minute. For damn sure, it was time for him to be heading for the house. He had to work in the morning. In a way, he regretted even coming; yet in another he was glad he'd made the effort. As usual, a woman had messed with his mind.

She sashayed back from the Ladies' and put both her hands on his shoulders. She leaned in and whispered, "It's kind of stuffy in here. Maybe you'd like to get some air?"

"Sure," he said, "let's go." Davis figured it would be easier to say goodnight if they were already out of the bar. He left his unfinished drink and a tip for Mike on the bar, swung off his stool, and followed Tanya across the floor. As far as he could tell, nobody was even looking at them.

As they stepped into the night, her face caught a narrow band of the bar lighting and Davis realized what a striking woman she was. With her long black hair, high cheekbones, and quick, alive, dark eyes, she could have been a model. He studied her sculptured lips, then swallowed an urge to kiss them.

As they began to stroll across the parking lot, she slipped her right hand into his left and he felt his heart begin to pump more quickly. Moonlight danced in her hair and the faint breeze caught her perfume and carried it to him. Davis felt loneliness flowing from his mind like a river and he wished they could walk this way all night. Only one thing bothered him, pricking him in the odd moments like a thorn, and that was why such a beautiful woman would be interested in him. He knew he was no movie star. Yes, some factor was wrong in that equation, but he was flying too high to worry about it at the moment.

Without speaking, they drifted across the parking lot, then crossed a grassy slice of ground until they found themselves stepping into a dark patch of chancy shadows beneath the thin line of second growth timber. She squeezed his hand, moving inside the curve of his arms as he turned to her. Without thinking, he tilted her chin up and kissed her, slowly and gently. Her lips were soft and warm and Davis felt a high tide of desire rising.

"Me thinks he rather likes me," the woman murmured against his chest. Davis felt the muscles in his arms tighten. "Okay, okay, enough big boy. You're squeezing the life out of me. Let me breathe, all right?"

"Sorry," he said, letting his arms go limp.

She rose on tiptoe and kissed him lightly on the lips. "That's okay, Davis. I'm not mad, but you don't know your own strength."

He'd already said sorry and didn't know what else to say, so Davis kept his mouth shut as he studied the way shredded moonlight painted her face, revealing hollows and curves darkened by shadows. Davis suddenly wanted to kiss every single one of the shadows. That wasn't all he wanted to do, either. Sure, he knew damn well those thoughts were wrong, but it had been so long. So damn long, he told himself. Way too damn long. Sainthood, he'd never volunteered for.

Tanya lifted a hand and a finger traced his jawline. "You know, Davis, you surprised me a moment ago."

"What do you mean, surprised you?"

She laughed softly. "I hadn't figured you for such an impetuous guy, that's all."

Davis had never thought of himself as impetuous, but he'd also never acted like this, at least not since high school. Maybe she had a point. "Hope I didn't offend you," he murmured.

"No, silly, you're just moving a little quick for me. Still, it's flattering to be kissed like that."

Davis wasn't sure what she meant by kissed like that, but he sure as hell wasn't going to ask. The problem was he didn't know what to do or say next. Every word, every action, seemed, one way or another, to be wrong. Safety seemed to lie in silence.

Clouds decorated the sky. One drifted across the moon and the shadows melded into darkness. Desire rose in him until he could feel his legs trembling. Davis wondered what she would do if he asked her for another kiss, and almost spoke the words. But he simply couldn't, not now anyway. Then the moon slid out from behind the cloud and he watched its light illuminate Tanya's face and knew he had to be going. He sure as hell didn't want to go, but wants didn't often factor in to the hard choices.

Davis had to swallow twice to get his voice to working, but, in the end, he got the words out. "It's late and I've got to work tomorrow. Need to be going."

"Honey, the night is young. Can't you stay a little longer?"

"Wish I could, but it's not young for a working man. Certainly not for an old working man like me."

Without warning, she lifted her face and kissed him, kissed him the way men dream about being kissed. "Call me tomorrow, Sheriff," she whispered as she pressed a slip of paper into his left hand. "Here's my number. What's yours?" She smiled. "Just in case of an emergency, you know."

Maybe someday he would listen to himself, at least to that inner voice writers were always talking about. But this was one more time he didn't. She punched the numbers into her phone. A pickup sorely in need of a new muffler pulled out of the parking lot. When it had disappeared, she said, "Remember, call me tomorrow."

Davis mumbled something about if he got a chance, kissed her lightly once more, then started striding across the parking lot. It wasn't until he got a good mile down the road that he remembered the "sheriff" comment. Davis worried that one around all the way to the house, questions niggling at the back of his mind. Maybe it was his age, but he seemed to be getting more confused by life every day.

Thirty-two

He came awake not knowing where he was, and, for the first several seconds, not even who he was. At first, all he could figure out was that he must have passed out in somebody's barn or shed, and he knew he'd better be getting the hell out before some farmer discovered him and called the law. As he worked his way to upright, he heard the restless stirrings of a sparrow in the rafters above him, remembered the sheriff, and eased back down. Pain began to radiate throughout his body and his mind flashed back to the recent beating. Birdman could feel his heart beating faster and his breath stirred thin and shallow in his throat.

He sat up slowly, tugged on his socks and shoes, then gimped to the door. Cracks in the walls and roof of the old shed let in enough light for him to pick his way among the tools, boxes, and sacks. He cracked the door open and pressed one eye to the opening. He knew it was unlikely that anyone knew he was out there, but once beaten, twice shy was Birdman's motto, especially when the one giving out the beating was Lawton Turner.

The only movements were those of shadows quivering in the gentle night breeze and Birdman felt his heart-rate slow as his breathing returned to normal. He looked skyward, trying to figure out from the moon's position how long he'd been asleep. Sleep was an uncertain visitor these days. Some nights, especially after a good fix, he slept the sleep of the dead; others—mostly when he was needing to get high—sleep refused to show.

The moon was well above the trees and Birdman figured he'd slept at least two hours, maybe three. That wasn't shabby, considering the beating he'd taken. Thank God for pain meds, Birdman thought as he meandered slowly across the open ground. He wasn't going anywhere in particular; he was simply too restless to lie back down in the shed.

What he needed was some crack, or a good joint, or even some more of those fine pain meds the docs over to Independence had given him. But he didn't figure the sheriff would have a stash hidden away somewhere. No, that wasn't in the cards.

Well, neither was staying in Pratt County. Not for the Birdman, anyway. Not with Lawton Turner lurking out there in the dark.

Now, Birdman knew his life hadn't amounted to much, and he was crystal aware he wasn't the brightest bulb in the pack. But it was his life, and he liked it all right. Most of it, in fact, was mighty fine.

Well, some of it.

Okay, so when he got high, life was good.

The rest of the time he was merely getting by, keeping both eyes peeled for the next high. Maybe he wasn't the poster child for Success In America. He was still a man, and he still had his rights, and he still knew his own mind. And right now, that mind was telling him to get the hell out of Dodge, or more precisely, out of Pratt County. Maybe what he needed to do was get the hell to Dodge. In the shadowy moonlight, Kansas seemed a much safer place than northwest Missouri. Of course, so did Mississippi, Montana, and Michigan—anywhere where Lawton Turner wasn't.

Why was Lawton Turner so hard on him?

Hell, that was easy. Even he knew the answer. Turner suspected that Birdman had ratted him out at some point. If he'd been sure, Lawton would have probably killed him—in the most painful way possible. No question about it, Lawton Turner liked to inflict pain. Birdman could testify to that.

Yes, he damn sure needed to get out of state, but...damn if there wasn't always a but sticking up to trip him. This time it was that he needed cash, big time, to make any sort of move. And he had zilch, zero, not one peso with which to make his break. For sure, he was screwed, again.

Birdman could feel his legs starting to go limber and he looked around for a place to sit. At first, all he could see were shadows tap dancing across open ground. Then he caught sight of an old Dodge Dart, half-hidden behind a building he figured had been a garage at some point. Birdman followed the moonlight trail to the vehicle, wobbling a time or two, but covering the few yards all right. Except for his legs starting to go and his head threatening to crack wide open, there was no need to hurry. The Dodge wasn't going anywhere.

It was up on blocks and, even in the moonlight, Birdman could see rust had established a strong foothold. He tugged on the driver's door and it creaked open. Sliding in behind the wheel, he closed his eyes.

For a moment, Birdman allowed himself the luxury of pretending he was actually going to fire up the engine and drive the old Dodge all the way to the Pacific. But he knew better. Life never had been that kind.

His life had been like that since that day when he was only three years old and his bratty sister, Missy—the one with buckteeth, had called him bird legs, just because he had skinny legs. And the stupid name had stuck. First, it had been Birdlegs, then Birdbrain, then Birdie, then The Bird, and now, at least to the Pratt County Sheriff's Office, Birdman.

He supposed it could be worse; still, he found the name degrading. He wondered if that was why he'd always been so hep on trying new thrills: beer and booze and weed and crack and meth. It was a thousand wonders he wasn't dead after all the shit he'd drank, smoked, snorted, injected—you name it Birdman Williams had done it.

A vision of his father drifted across the landscape of what was left of his mind. Arthur Williams had been a good man in a lot of ways. He'd always tried to work, although plenty of the jobs he worked had been crap: janitor at the jail, short order cook, night watchman at the ChemLo plant. Whatever it took to bring home some money, he did it. Did what was necessary to keep his family fed and clothed, and with a roof over their heads. His dad had never been a healthy man, battling a bad heart and crappy lungs all his life. He'd died young, shoveling cow manure at the stockyards. That had been over ten years ago and Birdman still missed him. Which was just one more piece of bad luck. Well, Birdman told himself, luck runs in streaks—good or bad—so his had to change sometime. Anyway, he sure as hell hoped so.

Birdman had always wanted to make his dad proud of him, although he hadn't done it often. He simply wasn't much of an athlete or a brain. Even his personality wasn't anything special. He was easy to get along with and didn't ask for a lot, but that was about it. One dream that had always stayed with Birdman was of him doing something heroic someday, taking some action that would make his dad smile, that would make all those other kids who'd gone to school with him at West View sit up and take notice.

But that was only a dream, and nightmares were more Birdman's forte. They were another reason he didn't always sleep so good. It wasn't particularly easy to close your eyes never knowing what might be hiding in the shadows of sleep.

Tonight, he knew all his aches and pains weren't going to make resting easy. Well, that was all right. He owed the sheriff for taking him in during his hour of need. Some men, most law, would have simply driven him to the county line, kicked his skinny ass out the door, and told him not to come back. But Davis Wells hadn't done that. Birdman figured he'd pay part of what he owed back by standing watch. Well, he'd sit while he watched, but that was okay. Birdman eased his head back against the vinyl, slit his eyes open, and let his vision drift across the night, across the big tree in the side yard, and the old farmhouse, and then across the field where sheep had once grazed, all the way to the road, white and shining in the moonlight.

Thirty-three

Willie and Tommy were waiting for Davis in his office when he finally rolled in to work. He set his coffee down on the desk, wondering why they were there. It didn't figure they were both waiting to chat about last night's ball scores. Davis hoped whatever it was could be told short and sweet—he was going on maybe five hours of sleep. Davis studied the deputies' faces, but couldn't read the news.

"What's up?"

The deputies glanced at each other, then Willie took a deep breath: "We've got another one."

Davis sat down and picked up his coffee. "OD?"

"You got it."

"Where?"

"About two miles west of where we found the Chisholm boy."

"Was this one in their car, too?"

"Yep."

Davis sipped his coffee. The hot liquid had a burnt taste, which suited his mood. "Who's the victim?"

Willie stretched his legs as he pulled his notebook out of his shirt pocket. "Victim's a Terri Powers. Twenty-three, bottle blonde, gray eyes, freckles." He lifted his eyes. "Looked like a nice kid, good clothes, no tats. No signs of needles. May be wrong, but I don't think she'd been using long."

"She lived on Ashley," Tommy said. "That's one of those new streets behind the Burger Boy. Homes there are running around in the low twos."

"Either of you know her?"

All Davis got was a pair of "Nopes." He was getting a headache—too little sleep, too much stress. Hell, he was just too damn old. Davis had been thinking about running for another term, but now another four years seemed like a life sentence.

He took another slug of coffee. Another death—just what he didn't need. "All right, let's get rolling. Willie, you do a complete shakedown of the crime scene."

"Roger."

"Tommy, you check with her employer. She was working, wasn't she?"

"At the Perlite plant. Second shift."

"Okay, check there and, if she was local, at her school. Any college?"

"No college, but she did go to West Pratt."

"There then."

A phone rang at the front desk and Claudia answered it. More trouble, Davis figured.

"Who's got the family details?"

Tommy slid an index card across the desk.

"Thanks. I'll take care of this." Somebody revved up a diesel out in the street. "This shit's getting old, gentlemen. Time to make something happen."

They both headed for their vehicles. Before they reached the door, the phone rang on Claudia's desk again.

Thirty-four

Something about the truck at the end of the driveway pricked at his memory. Davis remained outside his own truck, trying to remember where he'd seen the vehicle before. It wasn't new, maybe ten, twelve years old, with a few scratches and nicks, plus a major dent in the rear bumper. He couldn't place it, though, so he gave up and slogged up the driveway.

He stepped around a kid's tricycle and up on the shallow stoop. A television was playing inside, some goofy gameshow, blending with voices, conversations too muffled to interpret. He rang the doorbell.

The conversation stopped, followed by the sound of footsteps. Seconds later the door creaked open. A man's face swung around the corner and Davis remembered where he'd seen the truck. He knew the man, knew him fairly well.

"Dave."

"Hey, Davis. Long time, no see."

"Yeah, what's it been, two years?"

"Maybe longer. Probably the last season I coached American Legion. That would have been before my hip surgery, so say three years, three and a half." The man stepped back and swung the door open wider. "Come on in."

Davis pulled his hat off and stepped inside. After the glare of the sunlight, the room was dark and cool and he blinked as his eyes adjusted. Once his vision was better, Davis surveyed the room. He'd seen hundreds like it: a couch, recliner, television set, a shelf of photos and keepsakes. The very sameness saddened him.

A small child stared up at him from the floor. The child appeared to be about a year old and Davis wasn't sure if it was a boy or a girl, although, if he'd had to guess, he'd have said boy.

He turned to the other man. "Your grandchild?"

A faint smile pained the other man's face as he glanced at the child. "Yeah, my grandson, Tony. Just turned one."

The man looked away, then turned back to face Davis. His eyes were moist.

"Yeah, he's Terri's."

"I didn't recognize the last name."

"She got married a couple of years ago. A guy she met at college. College didn't work out for her and neither did he." Dave Cook leaned toward the little boy, smiled, then lifted his eyes. "Right there's the best thing that's happened to us."

"I'm sorry about your daughter, Dave. Real sorry."

The man opened his hands, then closed them. "Thanks." He pointed at the couch. "Have a seat. Figured you'd come. Not that I can tell you much."

Davis eased down on the couch. The little boy's eyes followed him and Davis smiled at the child. The child turned back to the blanket lying across his legs.

"I never did really know your daughter very well, Dave. What can you tell me about her?"

Davis could hear a microwave beep in the next room. Seconds later a woman appeared in the doorway, a cup in her hands. She glanced at Davis, then at the other man. Dave Cook fixed a smile on his face. "Honey, this is Sheriff Wells. He and I used to coach American Legion together. He's come about Terri."

The woman swayed, her dark hair swinging loosely, uncombed and tangled. Given the circumstances, Davis wasn't surprised. She set her cup down on an end table. Her hands were shaking.

"The sheriff was asking what we could tell him about Terri."

The woman stared at Davis for a second. Her lower lip trembled and he thought she was going to say something. Instead, she shook her head sharply, then crossed the floor quickly, stooped, scooped up the little boy in her arms and carried him out of the room without looking back.

"Sorry, Davis, this has been so hard on her, on both of us."

"I understand, Dave." His eyes felt hot, tired, and Davis rubbed at them. "This isn't the first overdose death. Appears somebody is peddling a really bad batch." He glanced at the man on the couch. "Now about your daughter?"

"Don't really know what to tell you. She was a good kid. Never really gave us any trouble." For a moment, the man looked at the television, then brought his eyes back to Davis' face. "Sure, she'd been through a rough patch, but it really wasn't her fault, and, besides, everybody goes through a few of those during their life."

Davis watched the man's eyes change as he realized how damn bad a patch he'd stumbled into.

"Was her divorce rough?"

The man on the couch appeared to be weighing how to answer the question. He toyed with the wedding ring on his left hand. "Not too bad. A few words were exchanged, sure. But basically, they were just a couple of kids who grew up and found out they didn't really like each other. He's paying child support. Works as a customer service rep for some tech company. Don't remember the name."

"How long have they been divorced?"

"Um, a little over a year."

"Had your daughter started dating again?"

The man rubbed a hand across his face. "Not really. Might have gone out for a drink with a guy a time or two, but mostly when she wasn't here with the baby she was with a couple of her girlfriends, girls she'd gone to high school with."

Mr. Cook shifted position on the couch and made a sour face. "That's where she told us she was going the last time we saw her alive.

Said she was going to meet a couple of girlfriends at that bar just outside of town. Oh, you know the name of it. Missouri something."

"Yeah, I know the place." Davis pulled a pen and notebook out of the pocket of his uniform shirt and scribbled a couple of words.

"She seem okay that night? Or was she especially happy? Or maybe upset about something?"

"Seemed normal to me. 'Course, women can usually fool me. But me and the wife, we've talked it over since it happened and neither one of us noticed anything unusual. And if Terri had been upset, Jackie would have noticed. Mothers are good about that sort of thing, you know?"

"Yeah, I know." Davis drew a picture of a star in his notebook. The star was lopsided, he noticed, wondering if that meant anything.

"Your daughter keep a diary, list of phone numbers, anything like that?"

"Not that I know of. Terri was a modern girl, kept everything on her phone, or maybe on her laptop."

"We'll want to look at both those, Dave. See if we can trace anything that might help."

"I figured. Got them all ready for you. I'll just go get them."

Davis watched his old friend walk out of the room. He put his notebook and pen back in his pocket and stood. Mr. Cook was already stepping back in the room.

"Here you go."

"Thanks, Dave. Here's my card. Won't bother you anymore, at least right now. If you think of anything you think I need to know, don't hesitate to call me. Anytime."

"I won't. Whoever is responsible needs to be punished. Sure hope you catch them soon."

"We're doing our best. I've got everyone working on the OD cases every minute they can spare."

The man opened his mouth, then closed it without speaking. Davis tried to smile, gave it up and turned. Sometimes words sounded hollow. This was one of those times.

Mr. Cook held the door for Davis. Halfway to his vehicle, Davis was struck by how close to home all the deaths were—seemed like every single one was someone he knew. Sure, he knew a lot of people in Pratt County, so the odds would be good he would know one of the people who'd OD'd on the bad batch, maybe two. But so many? That didn't seem right, or natural. Knowing all those dead people, or someone in their family, made him feel funny, like he was somehow at the center of the issue, or was, in some weird way, the cause. Then the image of Lawton Turner rose unbidden in his mind. In spite of the heat, Davis shivered.

Thirty-five

By the time Davis made the office, two more kids had OD'd. Actually, only one was a kid—a nineteen-year-old boy who lived in the projects. Davis recognized the name, though. He'd gone to high school with the boy's uncle, played baseball and basketball with him. They'd even gone fishing together a couple of times.

The other death was a thirty-one-year-old music teacher at the middle school. Her name was Nancy Clifton and Davis had played poker a few times with her brother, George. It was turning into a day from Hell—the kind of day West View had never experienced. Davis could feel his nerves beginning to rub raw and knew his temper was ramping up.

He washed down a granola bar with a cup of black coffee while he checked messages. He was reaching for the telephone when Claudia buzzed him.

"Mayor Gregory for you."

"Seriously?"

"Yep."

"And I guess he's his usual cool, calm, collected self?"

"You know it—not."

"Okay, but if I kill him, I'm pleading temporary insanity."

Claudia snickered and hung up. Davis hit the blinking button.

"Mayor."

"Davis, what the hell is going on?"

"Right the first time. Pure hell is what's going on."

"Two more deaths just this morning. We have to do something about it, and I mean like right away."

"We're working on it. I've got every man on the job and if we get one more fatality, I'm going to call in the state police."

"This all started with the Chisholm boy."

"I remember."

"Well?"

"What do you mean, well?"

"I mean, Davis, is that case solved?"

"You know damn well it's not, Mayor. But we're working on it. Crimes are solved in an hour only on television."

"Something needs to be done about all these drugs, and I don't mean the DARE program."

"We're working on it, Gregory. Working hard. Like I told you earlier, I've got every man out on the job. Just what the hell more do you want me to do?"

"Find out who's pushing all this bad dope and arrest them. Is that asking too much?"

It would have been diplomatic to respond to the mayor. He really wasn't a bad guy, but he could get on Davis' last nerve faster than anyone else. Davis was pleased he managed to not slam the receiver when he hung up.

~ * ~

Claudia grinned as Davis stomped out of his office. He closed his eyes and sucked in air. No use giving her a hard way to go. She wasn't responsible for the mayor. Davis took in a deep breath, then let it out as he opened his eyes. He didn't feel any better, but was a touch calmer.

"Any coffee left?"

She smiled. "Half a pot."

He crossed the room and filled a Styrofoam cup full. He couldn't be bothered by walking back to his office for his mug. Screw the environment. Well, not really, but he was in a pissy mood.

"That man is a jerk."

"Yes, but the citizens of West View love him."

"Hmm, as I recall, the mayors of Mayberry were all a piece of work, one way or another."

"Yep, but you aren't Andy Taylor."

Davis had to grin at that. "No, I wear a gun and Barney Fife isn't my deputy."

Claudia laughed. "True, but you're still one of the good guys."

"In my dreams."

Davis sipped at the coffee. It scorched his tongue. He made a face and tried to think about something besides his painful tongue. First, he wondered how Ellen was doing. Then, he wondered what Tanya was doing. One thing for sure—he didn't belong on the cast of Mayberry. Not even one of the bad guys on the show had been as much of a jerk as he was. A man whose wife was eaten up with cancer thinking about another woman was about as close to a snake as a human could get. Davis was ashamed, but he wasn't sure what he would do if push came to shove. A badge didn't always make a man good. Davis knew he had his weaknesses and he was tired, really tired of the way his life was these days. It might not be right, but he wasn't sure how long he could stand to wait for Ellen to regain her health. Down deep, his animal instincts were restless. That was simply a fact. Nothing more, nothing less. He tried to think of some place peaceful and quiet. When that didn't work, he gave Claudia a smile. One that felt funny on his face.

"Well, I'd better get on to nipping crime in the bud. I'm going to go and call Fred Hill."

"You'll make a hero yet."

"Bullshit," Davis said as he headed for his office.

Thirty-six

Fred Hill sounded like he was at the bottom of the bunker at the Greenbrier Resort in West "By God" Virginia. His words were muffled and Davis figured the man had one of his cigars clamped between his lips. Davis could almost smell the acrid smoke. The imagined scent brought forth a memory—a good one, for a change. His dad had smoked cigars.

Davis sensed his mind drifting and a heartbeat later it was forty years ago. His family was out for a drive, probably one of their Sunday ones: his dad, mother, sister, and his much younger self. Summer was in full bloom and the windows were down with his father's left arm hanging out the window, while the right one was draped over the steering wheel, a Dutch Masters poking out between his fingers. His mother was carrying on about the beauty of the countryside, while his sister was singing softly to herself.

All of them were gone now, and he was living with a wife who was dying, an epidemic of fentanyl-laced heroin, and a guilty conscience. Davis wanted to fire up his vehicle and start driving west, not stopping until he was beyond lost and no one knew him. Instead, he said, "Hello, Fred."

"Davis, what's going on?"

"You tell me."

"Suppose you're referring to our latest batch of corpses?"

"That's it. Know anything yet?"

"Yep."

Davis could hear the man puffing on his cigar. "And?"

Fred Hill cleared his throat. "And it's the same old shit. Somebody's laced heroin with fentanyl. There's a really, really, really bad batch out there. You'd better get your posse together and saddle up, bub." He snorted then, which Davis figured counted as a laugh for the old fart. "And I mean soon, Sheriff Wells. We've got one real badass dude out there."

"Yeah," Davis said, "and I've got a real good idea just who Mr. Badass is. Worse, I have a funny feeling this sicko is just getting started."

Thirty-seven

Ellen answered her phone on the third ring. Her voice sounded thick, groggy.

"Hey, it's me. How you feeling?"

"Maybe a little tired."

She sounded tired all right, and not just a little. "Hurting much?"

"Some."

Tension was building in his neck and shoulders. Davis could feel his delts tightening. They always did when Ellen was having one of her bad days.

"Need me to come home?"

"No, as soon as I finish reading the paper I'm going to go lie down."

"Can you handle lunch?"

"Sure, I've got some frozen Schwan's dinners."

"Yeah, you like the spaghetti and meatballs, right?"

"That one, and the turkey and vegetables."

"Cool." Outside, a flock of starlings was flapping around the top of the flagpole. Sunlight glittered off their wings and the metal pole. Old Glory hung limply.

"Another reason I called was to let you know I've got a witness hidden out in our old garage. He's a skinny, greasy-haired sucker who's just had the daylights beaten out of him. I think he's basically harmless, and he's under strict orders not to even come close to the house. However, keep all the doors locked just in case. And if you see him, call me."

"Who is it, Davis."

"He goes by Birdman. Oh, and Ellen...

"Yes."

"You might keep your pistol close."

Thirty-eight

"Fix me another drink."

"You sure? It's barely noon and you've already had two."

"When I want your advice, I'll ask for it. Now shut up and fix my drink."

"I'm just worried about you. You've been really tense the last couple of days."

"Tanya, I've told you and told you, I've got a lot on my mind. The new batch went out full volume two days ago and the shit should really be hitting the fan any minute." Lawton Turner smiled. "In fact, Davis Wells ought to be feeling like somebody just hit him up the side of the head with an anvil."

"Over a couple of druggies overdosing?"

"You're missing the point, Tanya. Every one of these druggies knows our good sheriff, or has kin who knows him. The people you and the rest of my folks have given, or sold, this batch to are important to Wells, one way or another. Every one of the deaths is going to hit him like a punch to the gut."

Outside the window, in the withering branches of a dying water maple, a bird chirped. Lawton Turner turned his head to search for the bird. He blinked against the light of the noonday sun, then found the bird, a small sparrow, on a lower limb that jutted out over what had once been a garden, but now was nothing more than patch of horseweeds and brambles. At the edge of the weeds, a rabbit twitched its nose as cloud shadows swept across the untended fields.

"I'll tell you this for sure, woman. Davis Wells is going to think the world is falling in on him, and then it is, up close and real fucking personal." Lawton Turner smiled, stretched, and closed his eyes. "Now bring me that drink."

Thirty-nine

Shadows sprawled eastward. The air had grown hot and still as the sun worked its way across Kansas, Colorado, Utah, Nevada, stretching for California, the Pacific, and the lonely islands in the deep, blue waters.

A man sprawled in the one of those shadows. One thrown by what had once been a henhouse, and was now beginning to tilt north toward Iowa. No chickens had lived there for years, but the man could still smell the birds and their feed and the dusty straw that still covered the floor. He rubbed his eyes as he shifted position, trying to get comfortable enough to go back to sleep. He'd managed to at least doze much of the morning, but sleep was elusive now, and he was starting to feel a need rising, and he knew, from years of experience, how long afternoon hours could be. Often, darkness brought some action, some relief, or at least the promise of some, but Birdman was half-convinced that afternoon hours frequently held more than sixty minutes.

He thought about eating a couple more of the crackers or one of the power bars the sheriff had left him, but he didn't see how he could face them at the moment. He felt a twinge in his gut and his brain shifted and he got his back firm against the wall of the henhouse and pushed himself upright. When his head quit spinning, he walked slowly down the side of the henhouse and eased his head around the corner.

If his cell phone had any juice, he'd call Stump, or Alec, or one of the Damron brothers. Birdman checked his cell phone again. Sometimes he didn't see things quite right, but, unfortunately, this time he'd seen reality. His phone was deader than the last Crusader.

Birdman eyeballed the road, but it was miles to town, and he wasn't anywhere close to sure that his legs could handle the trip. Plus, he promised the sheriff he'd hang around. Then, too, there was Lawton Turner to consider. That mother was evil, not to mention notorious for showing up where he wasn't supposed to be. But surely, even a badass like Lawton Turner wouldn't invade the Pratt County Sheriff's home. Would he?

Birdman shivered—Lawton Turner was one mean son-of-a-bitch, so off the freaking wall that no one could accurately predict what the creep would do. Birdman gave his phone a final look, then jammed the sucker down in the left front pocket of his jeans and eased on around the corner. It wouldn't hurt to take a look around. Wells hadn't told him he had to stay any one place in particular, only not go up to the house. However, the man hadn't said he couldn't look at the house.

Birdman stepped as quickly as he could across the open space between the henhouse and the wooden garage. After resting for a minute, he maneuvered around the backside of the garage, coming out only a few feet from what might have been the smokehouse back in the day. He wasn't sure, having spent most of his life in town, doped up, or behind bars. He'd seen pictures, though.

He looked to his right, across the sagging fence and a field that looked like it had borne crops not too many years ago, and then to an upslope of ground with a single white oak rising skyward at the crest. Above the oak a hawk floated, moving in ever-widening circles, while below, the native grasses shifted in the faint breeze drifting in from Kansas.

It was pretty enough land, he supposed, but his mouth was dry, and a tooth, one of the few he had left, had started to ache. Birdman could see that, if he didn't get some decent dope soon, he was about to be between a rock and a real damn hard place. He swallowed and forced himself to walk around the smokehouse, bent over, going as low and hard as he could, heading for a stack of firewood the sheriff had cut against the coming winter. Birdman hated winter and, in spite of the late summer heat, he shivered as he crossed the open ground.

Forty

As he eased his vehicle off the road, Davis had an eerie feeling he'd made exactly the same maneuver before. After a moment, he realized he damn near had. This car in front of him was less than two miles from where Mark Chisholm had been found. It was even on the same side of the road.

He braked to a stop, cut the engine, then sat and let both the dust and his nerve ends settle. His insides were all twitchy and pressure was building deep in his gut. Too many dead already, and it appeared to Davis it would be only a matter of time before there were more. What he wasn't sure of was whether it would be days, or hours, or minutes before the next death was phoned in. He had lived through similar cycles before and he recognized the signs.

Granted, he'd been slow in coming to the mark, but it seemed clear now that it was no coincidence that Lawton Turner had turned up at the same time as the bad heroin. Davis sat in his vehicle thinking about Lawton Turner, Birdman, Ellen, and, finally, Tanya, until sweat began to pop out on his face. Sunlight streaming in through the glass was turning the inside of the vehicle into an oven. Davis popped the door and swung his legs out.

Willie had his head stuck inside the cabin of the victim's car, and Davis strolled over and stood in the shade of a black locust until the deputy emerged.

"Hey, boss."

"Willie. Finding anything?"

The deputy wiped sweat off his face. "Nothing special. Just the usual—a few coins, a dirty napkin, a cracked CD, couple pair of sunglasses. Nothing special, except, well maybe..."

"What did you find? Come on, spit it out."

Willie tugged a Ziploc bag out of the front t pocket of his slacks. "Probably nothing, but..." He handed Davis the bag. "Here, take a look and see what you think."

At first, Davis couldn't see anything. Then he tilted the bag until the light caught it right and he could see a hair: a single, long, black hair.

"I figure it for a woman's."

"Just like with the Chisholm kid," Davis said, handing the unopened bag back to Willie.

"You'd better hang on to this. I'm running around like a wild man today. Just make sure it gets logged in and that we get the state lab to give it a good look. May not mean a thing, but then again it might."

A pattern was forming in his mind, but Davis couldn't quite pull it together. Years ago, he'd learned that whenever his brain didn't want to cooperate, he was better served to simply get busy doing something else, and if he'd really had a decent brainwave swirling, it would come to him uncoded at some point—an hour, a day, a week later. Same technique worked wonders for the tougher words in the Sunday Jumble in the *Star*.

Willie put the Ziploc back in his pocket. "Birdman doing okay?"

"Was when I saw him last night. Didn't see him when I left this morning." A crow started cawing from the tree line on the other side of the road. Seconds later, another answered. As Davis listened to them, he recalled his Uncle Ted always calling them raincrows—one word, like they only existed to forecast rain. He'd had a pet crow for a while. Kept him in a cage, with a light chain hooked to one leg. Uncle Ted named his crow Jim and taught him to say at least a dozen words. It hadn't been until Davis was grown that he'd realized old Uncle Ted had been making a political comment when he chose a name for his crow. By then Uncle Ted was dead and buried and Davis' memory was too fuzzy to figure out whether the man had been racist or sarcastic.

"You okay, boss?"

"Yeah, just thinking." His mind shifted and the dangling conversation line drifted back. "Anyway, I called Ellen to let her know about Birdman. Told her to call me if he started drifting toward the house."

"Think it's a good idea to have Birdman out to your place?"

"What do you mean? I figured him for harmless."

"Oh, I don't think he'd do anything." Willie rubbed at his face, then stared down the road as though he were looking for someone.

"Then what's the problem?"

Willie pulled a pack of smokes out of his uniform and tapped one out. He rubbed a hand across his mouth. "Don't know there is one, Sheriff. Only, I keep wondering about Lawton."

Davis didn't say anything, merely told him to go on. The crows had grown quiet and the afternoon had fallen as still as coffin dust.

"Now, we know he beat the hell out of Birdman, but he didn't finish him off and that bugs me. I mean we all agree Lawton is a badass motherfucker, but I'm also convinced he's no dummy." Willie stuck the cigarette between his lips and fired up his lighter. He blew smoke, staring through the haze with hooded eyes.

Davis made a face. "So the question is, why did he cut Birdman slack?"

"Exactly."

Davis peered across the road, through a gap in the tree line, to the field beyond. Wildflowers grew there, poking up among the sage grass and brambles. If she'd been there, Ellen would have been oohing and ahhing over the flowers. He probably should go pick some for her; he knew he wouldn't.

"What do you think, Willie?"

"Wish I knew. But I don't. All I can say is, I'll bet Turner's up to something."

"And it won't be good for us," Davis murmured.

"And it won't be good for us," Willie repeated.

Off in the timber, the crow started up again. A cloud drifted between Pratt County and the sun, and Sheriff Davis Wells watched a dark shadow slide across the wildflowers, the sage grass, and the brambles.

Forty-one

The wind had come up in the afternoon, rattling the cornstalks, buffeting the wild daisies and Queen Anne's lace along the fence row, whining under the eaves. A man lay on his back atop the brass bed in the bedroom, naked as the day he slid out of his mother's womb. Smoke curled from the cigarette in his right hand. His eyes were open, but unfocused.

In the bathroom, a woman stood before the mirror, casually brushing her hair, eyeing her smudged makeup, waiting for the man to speak. He always liked to talk after they'd made love, and she'd been sensing all day he had something on his mind, something he wanted to say. In the end he would say it, say whatever was on his mind. That, she was sure of. He always did. He was that sort of man.

She could still remember her mother telling her—she must have been seven or eight—that when she grew up she should get herself a man who knew what he wanted, a strong-willed man, a man who got what he wanted...one way or another. Tanya smiled—she reckoned that, at least in this way, she had minded her mother. Lawton Turner surely was a man who got what he wanted.

As though he had eavesdropped on her thoughts, Lawton Turner raised up on one elbow, ground out his cigarette in the green glass ashtray shaped like a maple leaf. Tanya had found the ashtray in the front room closet behind some old *Look* magazines stacked on a chair with three legs and a rotted-out seat.

"You know what to do, right?"

Tanya knew he could see her face in the mirror, so she smiled. "Yeah, you've told me three times already."

"Well then, you'd damn well better have it down pat. 'Cause we don't want no fuckups, not here, not now."

Lawton rolled out of bed and padded to the window. He leaned against the wall, easing his head around the remnants of the flowered curtains, looking out across the side yard. Lifted by the wind, a fine sheen of dust hovered all the way to the line of locusts planted years ago as a windbreak against the western winds. Beyond the locusts was a pasture going to seed, and then the ground fell away to Briar Creek. He wondered if there were still fish in the creek. Back when he been a kid he'd fished there: rock bass, redeye, and sun grannies.

He rubbed at his leathery face as he shifted his gaze toward the back of the old farmhouse. Between the outhouse and a shed that had fallen in on itself was a sagging clothesline. His mother had used a clothesline much like it. It was one of his final memories of her—hanging out the wash that last day, maybe an hour before she walked down to Turner's Pike sometime between breakfast and noon and caught a ride in a pickup truck with a man he'd never seen. The last image he had of her was the dust the pickup had spun up, shimmering in the slanting rays of an August sun. Lawton Turner blinked once, then turned around to face the woman.

"He needs to pay, you know? Davis Wells needs to pay and he's going to pay. No way in hell he's going to run me out of Pratt County, then get me put in the pen and not pay. Hell no, that son-of-a-bitch is going to have to pay, and pay big."

Too much booze and too many cigarettes had given him a headache, and Lawton massaged his temples. "If I had more time, I'd really string this out, killing one or two of his buddies a day until his nerves crack like a rotten stick. But I'm too well known in this county, and way too damn many people have seen my face to hang around much longer."

He took a step in the direction of the woman. "We got to make our move soon. Tonight, tomorrow night, the night after that at the latest. I can't take a chance on the wrong person seeing me and calling the law."

He shook his head. "I won't do it, Tanya, won't go back to jail. I'll shoot myself in the head before I let that happen."

He paused and she wondered if she should say anything. The boards of the old house popped in the heat of the afternoon and she could hear the humming of bees out in the yard. Just as she made up her mind to say something, he spoke again.

"Tell me again what you're going to do."

"Oh, Lawton. You're always making me repeat our plans."

"So? You'll be nervous, I know you, and you won't have any notes to help you remember. And this one we've got to get right." He leaned forward, his eyes fixed on hers. "Tell me, Tanya. Tell me now."

She caught the tone and eased the hairbrush down on the cracked vanity. As she maneuvered the eyeliner pencil, she said again what she'd already repeated three times that day. "I call the sheriff and try to get him to meet me out at the bar."

"And if he agrees?"

"Then we have a drink and dance a time or two."

"After that?"

She sighed, dropped the eyeliner pencil in her purse, molded her hair up on one side, and considered whether or not to use lipstick.

"After we dance, I let him walk me to my car and we kiss some, maybe fool around some, but not too much." She took a deep breath and rattled off the last of it, just like she had rattled off her history lesson back in high school. "Then I tell him I've got to go, and I take off quick before he can get to his car, and drive out to his place and meet you."

"Where?"

"I'll meet you just past his house, on the other side of the road, under that bunch of trees you showed me the other day."

"Then?"

"Then, I'll follow you through the old garden up to the house and do what you said."

"And what's that, Tanya? What are we going to do? Go ahead, tell me the rest."

Tanya didn't want to say the words, not ever. But she knew she was going to say them. Lawton would find a way to make her say them. Her mouth felt dry. She wished she had a glass of water, although something stronger would be better. She closed her eyes and told herself to be strong. After a moment she opened her eyes.

"We shoot them. I shoot the woman and you shoot the sheriff." She turned her head away from him, and looked across the bedroom toward the front door. Part of her wanted to run away, but the rest of her knew he'd never let her go.

"Why do you need me, Lawton? You know I'm not a good shot. Don't you have some friends? You're from this county, right?"

"Yeah, I'm from here, but all the guys I knew are in jail, been run out of state, or OD'd. That makes it you, baby. You're the only one I can count on. I'm depending on you, so don't let me down. Okay?"

Tanya shifted her line of sight until she was looking him in the eyes. "You'd better make sure with the first shot, Lawton. That man seemed pretty tough to me."

Turner snorted. "We'll see how tough he is when a three-fifty-seven round cuts through his guts." He started walking toward the bathroom. "I aim to gut shoot him and leave him to suffer and die in the fucking dust. You make sure you do the same with his wife."

"Why do we need to kill her, Lawton? She never did anything to you."

"Don't you worry about that. Just do what the hell I tell you. And remember, you shoot her first. I want him to know before he dies that she's going to die, too. That bastard needs to suffer. After all he's put me through, he surely needs to suffer."

The man made a sweeping motion with his right hand. "Now come here and give me a kiss, and make it a good one. A kiss for luck, for our best luck."

Forty-two

This must have been a pleasant place to live at one time, Tanya thought as she strolled across the front yard. A remnant of a white picket fence separated the yard from the weedy, graveled drive, and a burr oak shaded one corner. In its deepest shade were a pair of those metal chairs that rocked when you sat in them. Tanya vaguely remembered her Grandmother Thomas having green ones just like them in Little Rock when she'd visited her each summer, back before her grandmother had to go the nursing home.

Tanya eased down in the chair closest to the fence. She pushed a stray strand of hair off her damp forehead and closed her eyes. She needed to think. She needed to think real clear and she needed to do it now. Things were moving faster than she'd figured, faster than she liked.

She'd known Lawton Turner on and off for years, but they'd only really connected full-time after he'd got out of the state penitentiary in Idaho. He'd been honest about where he'd been for the previous eighteen months, but he'd told her for the truth that he was going straight and she was the very woman, the only woman, who could help him find the high road, and stay on it. She'd believed him then. That's what she'd told herself, anyway.

Of course, she should have known better, but every woman thinks, at least once, that she's the one woman who can change a man. Well, she'd taken her shot and, despite a couple of good months early on when he was working at the Roper factory and she was waitressing, now she knew better. From the start, Lawton had been broody, especially in the evenings after supper when he'd sat around for hours without talking, only smoking cigarettes and sipping now and then on whiskey.

Sure, she still cared for him, loved him maybe—if it came to that, but she didn't know if she could go through with what he had in mind. It was one thing to set the sheriff up, say for a good beating, but to help to kill him, well that was a damn big step. And as for shooting the sheriff's wife...she didn't see how she could go there. Not even for Lawton. Why, she didn't even know the poor woman. As far as Tanya knew, she'd never seen the woman. Any way you sliced that cantaloupe it was rotten.

Still, she'd learned the hard way not to cross Lawton. At least not without one hell of a good alibi, or a getaway plan. Tanya shifted in her chair until she could see him, bent across the motor of his Jeep, the hood up, doing something with a wrench. She knew next to nothing about car motors, actually not that much about cars. She wasn't even a particularly good driver. Lawton was, though, and she always felt safe riding with him. Actually, she always felt safe with him, at least before he'd gotten on this revenge kick. Now...

A gust of wind swirled up out of the fencerow and brushed her face. It was hot, dry, and reminded her of Arizona and her first, lost, marriage. She glanced down at her hands, frowning at the lines and the dark spot on the back of her left hand. Pushing forty, she wasn't young anymore. A few more birthdays and she'd be her mother, at least the way she remembered her mother. In spite of the late Missouri summer heat, Tanya felt chilled. She peered again at her at her hands, then turned her face to the sky. She'd have to make some sort of move, and soon.

Forty-three

The woman came haltingly awake, like she was coming out of a hypnotist's trance, shaking her head, blinking her eyes, licking her lips. The television was on—some home and garden show, and, from far off, came the thrum of a mowing machine. Closer, a fly buzzed stubbornly against the window glass. The woman propped herself up on one elbow and gazed through the glass at the side yard.

Shade from the house covered the yard, but she could see the grass needed cutting and the fence needed painting. A dead limb had fallen off the water maple and lay sprawled like some dead creature in the grass. Atop the fence a thrush swayed, feathers ruffling in the breeze.

Beyond the fence the land sloped away to the barn. A few cherry trees still lined the path that led to the barn. When they'd first moved to the farm there must have been thirty, maybe forty trees, and when they bloomed in the spring their blossoms had been beautiful beyond words. Now, less than a dozen trees remained, and they bore little fruit.

Stretching and yawning, Ellen Wells sat up. As she always did when she first awoke, she did her personal health checkup. This afternoon she felt no pain, her stomach was as calm as a Missouri farm pond in August, and her head was clear. For reasons she couldn't identify, she felt better than she had in weeks.

Biting her lip, she refused to let herself become excited. She'd had this happen before, only to feel lousy an hour later. Still, feeling good, even for a few minutes, was a blessing, and one thing cancer had taught her was to treasure those moments, make each of them count, treat every single one as a special gift.

Besides, she'd made a promise, made it to herself and to Davis—even though she hadn't told him—a promise to beat the cancer, a promise to live. Yes, life could be hard at times, and she allowed herself to wonder about their son for a moment—she couldn't handle any more than that—couldn't take it, couldn't stand thinking, wondering, worrying about him too much. Missing him was too dark a path to travel. She had to be strong. She had to be strong and pray, and maybe someday her prayers would be answered. She had to be strong for him, and for herself, and, of course, for Davis. He needed her, even if he didn't know it yet.

Thinking of Davis brought a smile to her face, and she closed her eyes and tried to breathe deeply the way the therapist had shown her. When she heard the old Seth Thomas on the mantle strike the hour, she opened them and began to look for her tennis shoes. The handyman on the remodel show on the television was talking about soft-close kitchen cabinets. The thrush swirled up off the fence and winged hard for the lilacs bush by the back door.

Forty-four

Birdman lay so still on the top of the rise of ground beyond the root cellar that he might have been a slice of the earth. His only movements were the faint, uncontrollable tremors that coursed down both legs and the minute quivering of the fingers of his right hand. He was so still that the hawk circling above might have thought he was asleep, but he wasn't. Birdman was wide awake. Wide awake with the need to get a fix of some kind.

Unknowingly, Birdman allowed a faint moan to escape his lips. It was too far for him to walk to town, he was still too sore from his beating to feel like moving much, none of his friends knew where he was, and his cell phone was deader than a Civil War tombstone. It had taken him the better part of an hour to work his way to his current perch, but he'd figured out his only hope was somehow getting the woman outside and then raiding the medicine cabinet or making a phone call. Judging by what he could see, the sheriff still had a landline. Birdman prayed it was a live connection. He was a man who prayed a lot, not that many of his prayers were answered. He tried to think when he'd last had a prayer answered, but his head still ached from the beating, and trying to think only made the pain worse. After a few brain twinges, he gave up and scooted closer to the edge of the mound.

Judging by the sun, the afternoon was growing old. He needed to act soon if the woman didn't cooperate. He could remember hearing that she was sick, but he didn't know what she had or how bad she had it. *Good Lord, what if she was bedridden?* Birdman shivered and eased another foot closer to the back door.

~ * ~

Shaky legs and all, Birdman was halfway down the slope when the back-porch door squeaked open. He dropped to the ground, glancing quickly to his left and right. Nothing—not one damn bush or tree to hide behind. Birdman pressed his face against the earth and prayed that whoever was coming out didn't look his way.

Smelling dirt and tasting grass, Birdman forced himself to count to sixty, slowly, before he raised his head a fraction of an inch.

First, he checked the back door, then let his line-of-sight slide to his right—off toward the west where a few high, thin clouds were drifting along the river. A crow cawed from the field behind him and cicadas hummed in the yard. He looked left in time to see the woman fading away over the hill, heading toward the barn. Nothing else moved in his field of vision, not in the yard, not in the fields beyond. Birdman shot a final glance toward the road, then pushed off the ground and began jogging for the back door.

At the door, he paused before turning the handle, listening. He winced as it squeaked open beneath his hand. Part of him wanted to turn and run, but stronger needs drove him on and he stepped inside, moving quickly across the back porch and into the kitchen.

A bowl half full of M&Ms sat on the table, and Birdman scooped up a handful as he drifted by. He'd hoped there would be a phone in the kitchen, but if there were, he couldn't see it. A rocking chair sat in front of some cabinets, next to a window that opened to the west. Birdman had always liked a rocking chair and for a moment he was tempted. But his nerves were singing, so Birdman kept moving, first into what looked like an old-timey parlor and then into a shadowy room full of heavy dark furniture that reminded him of his Grandmother Wilson's dining room. An aged Seth Thomas clock sat on the mantle and a strange, dark painting of a cherub and an owl hung on the east wall. The room smelled of dust, and, more faintly, of moth balls.

He was near the front of the house—he could hear the faint passing of a truck on the road—and Birdman took a careful look around, trying to figure out his next move. If he could help it, he didn't want to go upstairs, too much risk of getting trapped there to suit him, but he was running out of first floor footage. Out of the corner of his right eye, he caught sight of a door, crossed the floor and jerked it open.

At first, Birdman wasn't sure what the room was used for. It had a double bed, but also a day bed, a portable sewing machine, and a bookcase full of used books, mostly cheap paperbacks, a mix of romances and mysteries. A small television, which Birdman thought might have been new in the 1960s, stood on an old drop-leaf table in one corner, and above the table was a gun rack. Birdman glanced at the shotgun slung between two curved wooden U's, then moved on.

Six feet away, smack in the middle of a small round table, was what he'd been hoping, praying, to see. Whispering the number to himself, he double-timed it to the phone. An old .38 Police Special lay next to the phone, but Birdman was thinking about only one thing. His fingers were trembling as he dialed, but he could feel a smile crawling across his face.

Forty-five

His cell phone rang before he made New Market. Davis answered it without looking at the number.

"You gonna come see me tonight?"

He could feel his hands tightening their grip on the steering wheel. "This had better be an emergency."

She laughed. "Oh, it is. I'm positively desperate to see you."

He slowed for the caution light, then waved at an old woman sitting on her porch. "Don't call me unless it's really important, Tanya. I've got a job and I don't want to screw it up." The road bent west and he eased the wheel right a couple of notches.

"I'll come when I can get away." His voice sounded harsher to him than he'd intended it to, but the woman had pissed him off. Well, some.

Her sigh drifted to the satellite and back down to Pratt County. "You're married, aren't you?"

Davis swung out and around a Subaru doing forty. Someone who looked like a Vietnamese was driving. His eyes were focused straight ahead. "Yes, but..." Davis couldn't think how he wanted to finish the sentence, so he let it die on the vine.

"But what?"

"But nothing. Never mind. I'll come tonight if I can. If not tonight, soon."

"The sooner the better, Davis. I miss you. I really miss you. And I really am rather desperate, you know?"

He could hear the longing in her voice. It sounded as real as a heart attack. Hell, he was a touch desperate himself. But he had a job to do, and a wife who...who what? Needed him? Maybe. Wanted him? Not in a long time. Who what? Now that was a damn good question. What did Ellen really think about him?

Or maybe the better question was: did Ellen think about him at all? Of course, she had plenty on her mind with the cancer and the treatments and all the lousy stinking side effects.

But, like every quarter you ever handled, there were two sides. And the other side to that coin was that absence makes a man wander. At least his mind. Davis' mind had, anyway. Sure, he knew it was wrong. And lust was supposed to be a sin. Well, in his book, loneliness should be classified as one, too.

Davis rolled up the hill where the Chevron station had been in business for as long as he could remember. If you were female, or a handicapped male, they'd still clean your windshield for you. Deek Wilson and Bert Wilcox were standing out front and he flicked the siren and waved.

"I'll come if I can. Only don't count on it. Not for certain, see?"

"A girl can hope, can't she?"

"Guess anyone can hope."

"See you soon, baby," she said and blew him a kiss.

Davis clicked the phone off and floored the accelerator.

Forty-six

In the end he went. He knew he would. Davis had never claimed to be much of a student back when he was in school, but one thing he'd learned real early on was that imagination beat the crap out of discipline, every time.

Not that he went right away. First, he went back to the office and caught up his paperwork, returned a call to the mayor, who was as much a pain as ever, and gave three noncommittal answers to four questions from the *Chronicle*. Just before he hung it up for the day, Davis met with Willie, Tommy, and the rest of the officers and beat around options on the fentanyl crisis until he worked up a pounding headache.

Not that all the talk made things any clearer. But at least everybody was on the same page when he ended the meeting. And they all agreed, it was time to put the full court press on every dealer, user, and source they had in Pratt County. Plus, they all promised to keep an eye out for Lawton Turner. Willie had the late shift and said, if he wasn't too busy, he'd work up a game plan for the office to use by the time the first shift arrived. What Davis really longed for was a day without another fentanyl death. He needed time to clear his mind and do some hard thinking. Lawton Turner's name kept floating to the surface and Davis had learned years ago not to ignore messages like that.

On the way home, Davis stopped and got Birdman another box of fried chicken from the Colonel, a twelve-pack of water, a six pack of Coke, and a bag full of junky snacks. He couldn't have his special witness starving.

Ellen was asleep on the couch when he got home, so Davis gathered up his purchases and strolled down to the garage. All he found was dust, darkness, and a few rudimentary designs drawn on the dirt floor. Apparently, Birdman had artistic urges.

He put all the goodies on a sack of grass seed and stepped back outside to see if he could track down his wandering witness.

Dusk was drifting in from the east and the air had gone purple-gray in the swales where the barn swallows were making their evening swoops. Davis figured he'd put enough fear in Birdman to keep him away from the house, and, since he didn't figure Birdman was the sort of man to wander in the fields and forests, the barn was the obvious place to look.

Davis' grandfather had milked his cows in the barn, and stored hay and corn there. He'd also stabled a couple of horses there when Davis had been a kid. He could vaguely remember riding a buckskin around the barn lot a couple of times.

After Grandpa passed, his dad had at least kept the barn fixed up and he'd had it painted a time or two, even patched the roof once. Davis knew he'd let the barn go downhill. Even the path to the barn was getting overgrown. He was sorry for not doing better, but both time and money always seemed to be in short supply. He picked his way through a gathering dusk thick with memories.

Fireflies had started flickering on and off by the time he made the barn. Davis strolled into the milking parlor, startling a black and white tomcat who was trying to establish squatter's rights. He rubbed up against Davis' legs, but Davis shooed him out and hollered for Birdman.

He answered the third time Davis called his name.

"Up here, Sheriff. Up in the hay loft."

"What the hell you doing up there?"

"Been watching the birds, but now they're either settling down for the night or out hunting their supper."

"Well, it's about time you started settling in for the night, so come on down. I've got you some supper back in the garage."

"Sounds good," Birdman said, and in a few seconds Davis heard the creak of the ladder that had been nailed to one wall of the barn.

Even in the poor light, the witness didn't look so hot. His face appeared hollowed out and his right eye twitched incessantly, plus he was a touch unsteady on his feet. He stumbled once and, when Davis grabbed an arm to steady him, he could feel the trembling.

"You all right?"

Birdman looked at Davis out of his good eye. "Making it, I reckon." He gave Davis a sickly grin. "Sure could use a fix, boss."

"Tough luck on that one," Davis said. "Wouldn't do for me to be supplying a witness with drugs." Davis tugged on his arm. "Come on, let's get back to your quarters. Got you some more fried chicken."

He grinned and mumbled a couple of words Davis couldn't catch. Davis didn't bother asking him to repeat them. They slogged up the hill together, panting, walking out of step. Darkness was building by the minute.

Off to the north, in what had been pasture in his dad's day, Davis could hear quail—the male calling and the female answering. Funny, he thought, it used to be that way between men and women. Only not so much these days. Tanya was a good example of the change.

Thinking about her made him want her, and that was no good, so Davis gnawed on his lower lip and picked up the pace. He could hear Birdman groaning behind him, but Davis didn't care. He had his own demons to deal with. When you got right down to it, he thought, every man had demons. Only, if experience was any sort of a teacher, some tried to escape them, while others welcomed them. So far, he'd simply lived with his.

"You hungry?"

"Damn near starved. Guess maybe you ain't brushed up on the prison regulations lately, Sheriff, but a prisoner is supposed to get three squares a day."

Davis smacked Birdman on the back. "Only trouble with that is, Mr. Attorney, you ain't my prisoner. You're my guest."

"Who sleeps in the garage."

"So? It's dry in there and, at least as far as I know, Lawton has no clue where you are."

"He better not."

"Yeah, well, here we are. Now, you'd better get in there and eat your chicken and taters while they're at least lukewarm." Davis took a long look at Birdman's face. Bones poked at the skin and a rash covered one patch of his left check. However, his eyes were steady and his jaw firm. "Everything go okay today?"

"Yeah, guess so. Only it was one helluva long day. Thought a couple of times I was going to die of boredom."

"Boredom won't kill you, hoss, but Lawton Turner just might. You'd best lay low for a few days until we can lay our hands on him."

"He's a hard man to hold."

"Yeah," Davis said, "I know." He pointed at the box of chicken. "All right, Birdman, you get in there and eat before the grease sets up. I'd better get to the house and check on my wife."

Davis gave Birdman his hard lawman look. "You haven't been aggravating her, have you?"

"No, sir," Birdman said. "Kept my ass in the barn or down by that cruddy pond all day."

"Good deal. I've got to go. I'll try and bring you some breakfast down in the morning."

"Sounds good, and, if you get a chance..."

"What?"

"Can you bring me a couple of magazines, or even a book when you come? Just to pass the time, you know."

"See what I can round up." Davis turned and headed for the door. "Catch you in the morning," he said over his shoulder.

"Thanks, man," Birdman called back. "You sure are good to me. Whole lot better than anybody else, except my mom, back when she was living."

"Just doing what I can."

"I'll pay you back someday, Sheriff. Swear and promise."

Davis doubted that. In the law enforcement game, a man heard bullshit every day and Birdman had been bullshitting everybody, including himself, for so long he probably believed whatever line he was spouting. Davis paid him no more mind than the blowing wind.

Like the poem said, he had miles to go and promises to keep. Maybe his witness said a few more words. Only Davis wasn't listening—not really. He was shifting mental gears, readying himself to head hard for the house in the swallowing darkness. The feeling that he was late for something important ran through him like a dose of salts.

Ellen was sitting in the rocking chair in the kitchen. As the screen door screeched, she looked up from the newspaper.

"You're late."

"Busy day, plus I had to tend to my witness." Davis crossed the room, bent and kissed her cheek. "How you doing?"

"Better this evening."

"Hungry?"

She smiled. "Maybe a little."

Davis leaned against the counter and closed his eyes for a second, letting waves of tiredness wash over him. Getting too old for this job, he thought, not for the first time. "What'd you have for lunch?"

She looked away for a moment, then down at the floor. "The rest of the chicken salad. And a banana. Well, most of it."

Davis smiled as he put on his cheerful face. "That's not bad. What would you like tonight? I'm pretty handy with a can opener, you know."

Ellen let her head fall back against the chair. "You pick it, Davis. I'm not really feeling like anything in particular."

"Take your medicine today?"

"Yes, of course."

"You know what the doctors said about being sure to take the right dosage at the right time."

"I know, I know." She shut her eyes and he wondered what she was thinking about, or if that was simply her way of shutting him out. Her eyes fluttered open. They fixed on his.

"It's late, Davis. If you want to cook something quick, I'll eat it. Otherwise, I'll eat some peanut butter on crackers and go on to bed."

Just then, the old Seth Thomas in the parlor started up. Davis counted nine. Later than he'd realized. No wonder they were both tired—they weren't kids anymore. And instead of fixing her something to eat, he was standing around blabbering. Sometimes he got so pissed at his own stupidity. He hurriedly washed his hands and did his best imitation of his Uncle Edgar, who'd run a grill down in Dallas for years.

When he was a kid, maybe thirteen or fourteen, his folks had put him on a bus one summer and Davis had gone down to Dallas and stayed with Uncle Edgar and his wife, Sue, for a couple of weeks. He couldn't remember now why he'd gone. Uncle Edgar and Aunt Sue hadn't had any children of their own, so maybe they'd wanted to see what it was like to have a boy around the house. Or maybe his folks had simply wanted a break from an overactive youngster. Whatever the case, he went to Texas for two weeks, where he'd gone to work every day with Uncle Edgar at the grill.

Actually, his uncle was more than the owner of the grill. He was also, at least much of the time, the waiter, short-order cook, and dishwasher. Davis vaguely recalled an old lady who helped at the counter during rush hour, and an image was stuck in his mind of a black man with a game leg helping with the dishes and mopping the floors and such. But that had been a long time ago and his memory wasn't what it had been.

He shook his head and channeled his inner Uncle Edgar. In ten minutes, he had a late supper on the table: cream of chicken soup (out of a can), a tossed salad (out of a bag), a pair of turkey sandwiches, and a bowl of blueberries and blackberries. Haute cuisine it wasn't, but it wasn't bad for a tired old sheriff.

Ellen ate a bowl of soup and more than half her sandwich. He ate like a farmhand. By the time they'd finished, she was on a downward spiral and he helped her to bed.

Davis had the sense that she wanted to talk, but was simply too tired. He kissed her eyes closed and went back to the kitchen. It was after ten before he got the food put up and the dishes washed. Part of him wanted to stay home, and he knew he should listen to that side of the conversation.

But he had urges, strong ones, and sometimes a man simply had to go with where his mind takes him. Davis wrote Ellen a note, propped it against the toaster, and stepped out into the night.

Forty-seven

The crowd was thin, the smoke thick, and the music so slow it sounded like it was on its last legs. Tanya picked up her drink, then eased it back down on the bar. She checked out the room before peering at her watch. In the dim light, the numbers were hard to see, but she finally made them out. Almost eleven. Shifting in her seat, she closed her eyes.

Not for the first time she wondered what she was doing here. Of course, she was here because Lawton wanted her to be, but that didn't make it right. Even if she didn't always stay on the legal side of the line, she knew right from wrong—and what Lawton wanted to do was wrong. Killing that sheriff was something bad, really bad, far beyond anything she'd ever stooped to do. He'd only been doing his job when he ran Lawton out of the county. Plus, he seemed like a nice guy. He'd always been polite with her, at least. Besides, he liked her, she could tell.

None of that would make any difference to Lawton. She knew Lawton was going to do what he'd said. He was going to make the sheriff suffer and then was going to kill him. Lawton Turner never promised one thing he didn't deliver.

Which put her in a bad spot, no matter how you considered it. If she helped Lawton, she'd be an accessory to murder. If she didn't... Well, she'd probably be dead before the week was out, her body jammed in a haystack, tossed down a ravine, or burnt to a crisp. No doubt about it--she was in a bad spot.

She glanced at her watch again. A quarter after eleven. The door swung open and her head swiveled on her neck. But it was only a couple of farm boys clomping in, throwing their heads back and laughing. She turned back, lifted the glass and drained it. She'd give Davis until midnight—then she was gone. There would be another night.

Forty-eight

She came wide awake, her mouth agape, breathing heavily, sweat beads dotting her upper lip. Ellen Wells sat up in the bed feeling she'd somehow missed something important. Silently, she ran a quick inventory of her medical issues. Everything seemed all right—better than normal, in fact. She flipped off the cover, swung her feet out on the floor, and padded to the window in her gown.

Moonlight salted the lawn and the trees. Shadows lay still and deep. Ellen held her breath and listened, but all she could hear was the ticking of the clock on the mantle, and more faintly, the drip of a faucet somewhere in the house.

For once, she didn't feel tired and she considered fixing herself some tea and toast. Then she thought of Davis, cocked her head and listened for him. When she couldn't hear him, she slipped on her robe and house shoes and went to look for him.

Three minutes later, she found his note stuck on the microwave. Another late-night emergency. She swallowed her disappointment. Since she was having one of her good spells, she'd hoped they could have a good talk, share some time together, maybe even a little more.

Ellen ran the palm of her left hand across her face, then turned and headed for the cupboard. She'd have that cup of tea after all.

Forty-nine

For the tenth time that night, Birdman wished he had a watch. Donnie Hillock was supposed to be bringing him a rock by eleven o'clock and it sure seemed later than that to Birdman. He looked skyward, searching for the moon. Not that it would tell him much— he'd never been one to study the night skies—but at least he might get some sense of whether it was late or early.

The moon was up all right, playing hide and seek among some scuttling clouds. When the clouds parted, Birdman could see a few stars. One of them was extra bright and he guessed maybe that was one of the planets—say Venus or Jupiter. Seemed like they'd studied them in school, maybe seventh grade. Anyway, if he were remembering correctly—always a doubtful proposition—one of the planets was extra bright at night.

Hell, what did that matter? It was late and he was supposed to meet Donnie by the mailbox. If they missed connections, Donnie was going to leave it in the mailbox. Birdman had seen the sheriff get the mail earlier, so he shouldn't have to worry about an interception. Besides, he'd heard the sheriff drive out an hour or so ago. Some hot case, he figured. That made him think of Lawton Turner and Birdman felt his nerves starting to sing.

Lawton Turner basically terrified him. Even the thought of that badass caused his guts to hurt.

Birdman shook his head, sniffed, and struggled to his feet. He was bad to nod off—maybe he'd been asleep and missed Donnie. He took a tentative step; he was starting to hurt for a fix pretty bad and his legs were going all shaky. He sure as hell hoped he could make it to the damn mailbox. Surely he could do that. Fate wouldn't be so cruel.

The first step wasn't bad, so he took another, followed by a third. By the time he reached the driveway, he could feel the strength flowing back into his legs and shivered a little inside himself. Amazing what a promise will do for a man.

Just to be on the safe side, for he was usually a cautious man, Birdman took a quick look around. Moonlight coated the gravel before him and the shadows beneath the trees were still. All quiet on the farmyard front, Birdman joked to himself. As he started to turn and step off down the drive, a glimmer of light inside the house caught his eye. Birdman sucked in air and looked quickly for the sheriff's vehicle. Still gone. That was good, but what the hell? Birdman massaged his forehead as he tried to think. Thinking didn't always come easy these days.

After a few seconds, he decided the sheriff's wife must be up. Awful late to be up, but then women were always surprising Birdman. He had never understood them, never figured out what they were going to do. Even Sandra Crosswaite, who he'd sorta shacked up with for a while before she OD'd on pills a couple of years ago, had been a source of confusion for Birdman.

Now what was he supposed to do? What if she came out of the house and saw him walking down the drive? The moonlight was sure bright enough for that. Hell, she might shoot him, or at least call the sheriff. And the sheriff had given him strict orders.

From distant fields he could hear the lowing of cattle, and in that instant Birdman realized he was standing in open ground with the moon shining down on him like a spotlight. Moving with all the speed he could muster, he stepped into the shadows and leaned against the plank fence that separated the drive from the yard. He'd have to do some thinking, that was for sure. What was it his Uncle Andy had always said? Oh yeah, something about weighing all his options. Birdman felt his insides knotting up. Fear, or needing a fix? Either way, it was damn unpleasant. What the hell was he going to do? What the hell...

Fifty

Lawton Turner took a final drag off his cigarette and ground it out against the brick wall of what had once been Turner's Five and Dime. The dying summer sun had gone down twenty minutes before and only a faint lavender afterglow remained. All the cars and trucks that were moving had their headlights burning and birds twittered drowsily in the trees that had grown up between Turner's and the vacant lot where Croley's Used Cars had operated back in the Nixon years. Lights still burned in Hart's Drug Store, Wilma's Coffee Shop, and the Swifty Mart, but most of the buildings, at least the ones that weren't vacant, had gone dark. Only a few people, mostly men, still strolled the sidewalks.

Lawton watched a West View patrol car roll by, then pushed off the bricks, strolled west and casually made his way into the deeper shadows beneath the trees. He paused once to survey the street. But nothing moved on either sidewalk, and Lawton walked toward his Jeep parked at the back of the old parking lot. The pavement was cracked and potholed, and with the light so lousy, Lawton picked his way carefully, making sure of the surface before setting his feet down. One of the last things he needed was a sprained ankle.

Lawton cranked the motor, then paused, going over in his mind what he needed to do and when he needed to take action. He'd gone over everything several times before, but it never hurt to do a final mental run-through. It was a process that had served him well over the years.

The radio was tuned to a country oldies station and Porter Waggoner was singing about the cold hard facts of life, which Lawton thought was right damn appropriate because he aimed to teach Davis Wells a few of those—right before he blew his brains out.

Porter finished being locked up in his cell, which Lawton had no intention of letting happen, then Hank Snow started singing about all the places he'd been, and Lawton followed along, making a mental checkmark of all Hank's towns he'd passed through. Before the night was out, Lawton aimed to be headed for some new territory, as Missouri figured to be too hot for him in a few hours.

Well, that would be all right. He would have paid his debts and he'd never seen much of Arkansas and nothing of Louisiana. Once he got south of Kansas City, he'd stay on 71 all the way through Neosho, Goodman, and Pineville, all the way to the Arkansas line. He'd spent most of the last few years west of Missouri: Kansas, Oklahoma, Nebraska, Colorado—that sort of territory, and he figured the law would look for him there first. He grinned; he'd outsmarted John Law before and he would again.

Lawton glanced at the dashboard clock and turned the radio down. Time to roll—he wanted to be in place in plenty of time. He'd have to wait some. That was okay. He'd been waiting the better part of five years; a few more minutes wouldn't hurt.

He shifted into drive and eased his foot off the brake. As he motored through the thickening darkness, he rolled his window down and let the sounds of the Missouri night drift in. At the edge of Main Street, he braked to a stop to listen. He could hear a faint murmur of voices, the low rumble of a motorcycle a couple of blocks away, a door slamming shut, and then the call of a night bird. When the bird's call was answered, Lawton shifted into drive and pulled onto the street.

Fifty-one

Davis Wells shifted into park, popped the door, and swung his legs out into the night. As his feet hit the gravel, he checked the time. Eleven-fifteen—later than he thought, wanted. He hitched up his pants and started marching. He could hear the gravel crunching beneath his feet, a faint murmuring of voices out in the dark, and the throb of a truck motor from the highway, all mingling with the shrill voice in his head. The one telling him to turn around and go home. He ignored them all and pushed open the door to Missouri Wet.

The hour was late and the crowd was thin, and it took him less than a minute to find her. She was sitting at the bar, staring down at her drink, the faint light shimmering on her long black hair. He took a survey of the room. Without a doubt, she was the most beautiful woman in the bar. Her long dark hair framed her face perfectly and the whiteness of her slender neck stood in sharp contrast to the dimness of the bar. He watched her well-formed fingers curl and uncurl around the glass, imagining how they would feel against his bare skin. Still, he hesitated, torn between the voice in his head and the desires that drove him. Then she turned her face toward his and smiled and he started across the dimly lit floor.

"You're awfully late. I was beginning to think you weren't coming."

"Sorry, it's been one of those nights," he said as he slid onto a stool. "I've been busy."

Tanya ran the fingers of her right hand down his left check. "You do look tired, baby."

"That's because I am. It's been one helluva a week."

"Would a drink help?"

Davis turned and studied the bottles lining the wall above the mirror behind the bar. He sighed, then buried his face in his hands. After a moment, he lifted his head. "You know, maybe not tonight. I'm tired and I've got to roll hard tomorrow."

He looked at the woman then, his eyes suddenly alive. He tapped the glass holding her drink. "Why don't you finish that, and maybe we could take a walk, get some fresh air."

Tanya smiled. "Think I've had enough. Why don't you finish it for me?"

Davis hadn't wanted a drink, but he considered it now. No one at the bar he knew. At least no one he recognized in the dim light. One wouldn't hurt. Hell, the glass wasn't even half full. He lifted the glass, tilted his head back, and downed the drink in one long swallow.

The drink was too sweet for his tastes, but it had a kick. Almost instantaneously he could feel the warmth blossoming in his stomach. He sat the glass back on the counter and made a face.

"Damn, that was nasty. How do you drink it?"

The woman responded, but Davis wasn't listening. Two county commissioners were walking in the door and suddenly Davis didn't feel like conversation. He turned away from the door and eyed the woman behind the bar. She wasn't the regular and he didn't recognize her, but she moved like she knew what she was doing. He wondered where Mike was. Then he wondered what his next move should be. A hand caressed his neck.

"You okay?"

"Yeah, sure. Only let's get out of here." Davis thought for a second. "You go on. I'll join you in a minute. Wait for me at the end of the parking lot, where you parked before."

The woman gave him a look he couldn't read, picked up her bag and headed for the door. Davis spent a couple of minutes going over the case in mind, then tossed a five on the bar and started for the parking lot. He kept his eyes focused dead ahead. If anyone spoke, he didn't hear them.

Fifty-two

Off in the distance, off to the west, off toward Kansas, he could see headlights. For what seemed like forever, he'd been waiting by the mailbox. Birdman glanced skyward. Yeah, the moon was higher, but not by much. Time dragged like thick rope through wet sand when a man was needing a fix. The headlights disappeared as the car went down a dip, only to reappear when it crested the rise a mile away. Birdman heard the whine of the car's motor and he felt his body quiver with anticipation.

What with it being the middle of the night and no traffic, he'd been standing in the middle of the road, and now Birdman wobbled over to the mailbox and leaned against it, keeping his eyes fixed on the headlights that were closing fast.

In the stillness, he could hear his stomach growl and wished for some more of the chicken the sheriff had brought him. For a lawman, Davis Wells was all right. For sure, he treated him better than his own family had the last few years. He'd have to find a way to repay. Birdman didn't have a clue how he'd ever do that. Maybe he'd get a tip sometime and pass it along. Help the sheriff catch a badass or save a life. Hey, you never knew. Birdman had seen sights no one would ever believe.

The car began slowing and an image of Lawton Turner flashed across Birdman's brain and his legs started to really shake. Then he got a grip on his imagination and told himself no way would Lawton Turner risk driving by the sheriff's house. Immediately, a calmness flowed through his mind, and Birdman felt his lips form a smile as the car came up the final grade and began easing over toward the mailbox.

Seven seconds later, Birdman could make out a hazy face behind the windshield and then he could see for certain it wasn't Lawton Turner behind the wheel. The car rolled to a stop beside Birdman and the driver powered the window down. Birdman leaned in.

The face wasn't one he knew, and Birdman leaned back. The dude didn't look like trouble, but these days a man didn't need to take chances. Birdman started to say something, thought better of starting anything, and pressed his lips together. He wasn't smiling anymore.

The man behind the wheel tilted his face up. "You Birdman?"

"That's right, but who are you? You sure ain't Donnie Hillock."

"Naw, I'm his cousin, Joey. Donnie got tied up and told me to give this to you." The man thrust out a hand.

For a second, Birdman thought the hand was empty. Then he shifted the angle of his head and he could see a small plastic baggie. He reached out and took it. It didn't feel right and it didn't look right. Birdman popped it open and ran a couple of fingers inside.

They closed on what felt like a cigarette and Birdman pulled the object out and held it up to the best moonlight he could find. The damn thing was a cigarette. A damn weed stick. He felt sick.

"Hey, man, this isn't what Donnie was supposed to send. You got another baggie in there?"

"No, buddy, that's all I got. Donnie said to tell you all kinds of shit is going down with the cops and he couldn't lay his hands on anything else tonight."

"Well, that sucks."

The man behind the wheel leaned closer. "What you see is what you get. Better be damn glad you got that. Cops are really cracking down tonight. I took a big chance coming out here. Wouldn't have done it, but I owed Donnie one."

He figured he knew the answer, but Birdman asked anyway. Never assume was his motto. "Why the crackdown?"

The man sniffed like he was coming down with a cold. "Don't know for sure, but Donnie heard there was some bad shit making the rounds. Heroin laced with fentanyl is supposedly killing off people right and left. We figure they're looking for the source."

Yeah, and that's Lawton Turner, Birdman said to himself, glancing up and down the road as though the bad man himself might be marching his way. "Well, that don't help me none, does it?"

"Tough luck, dog, but that joint in your hand is all you're getting tonight. At least from me." The man turned his face back to the road before him. "I got to roll, man. Later."

Birdman watched the driver shift into gear and then dust was rising in the moonlight and all he had to show for all his trouble was a single lousy joint. Birdman felt like crying.

"Later, my ass," he mumbled to the dust, turned back toward the house, and started up the driveway. Still, he told himself, a joint was better than nothing. If nothing else, it would relax him some. Maybe enough so he could even grab a couple of hours of good sleep. Birdman trudged on, his moon shadow floating before him.

Fifty-three

Days could be long, but the nights were often infinitely longer. This was one of those nights.

She'd came wide awake out of a deep sleep a few minutes earlier, feeling refreshed and without pain. It had been so long since she'd been without pain that the sensation felt strange. It wouldn't last, certainly not for long, and she was determined not to waste the moment. She slipped on jeans, shoes, and her knock-around top. Dressed, she started moving.

As she entered the kitchen, she sensed desire welling up inside her and wished Davis were there. But no, as so often happened lately, he was out on a case. While she admired and respected his dedication, she sometimes wondered if she'd made a mistake marrying him. It was one thing to love someone; it was another to love their image in their absence. Ellen's mind drifted across fading sepia images as she poured herself a glass of sweet tea.

She drank her tea standing up at the kitchen window, staring out at the yard and the old garden and then up to the sky where the stars seemed to burn white hot. The moonlight that sprawled across the ground looked cool, however, and a longing to walk in it rose until it could not be denied. She turned, placed her glass on the table, and went to change. As she started into the parlor, she remembered Davis' warning to be careful and thought of the revolver.

Fifty-four

He found her standing in the shadows of a line of scraggly trees that marked the eastern end of the parking lot. She was leaning against the trunk of a tree no thicker than she was. When he was a step away, he stopped, still in the deep shadows, and waited. He'd come this far, but couldn't find it in himself to take that final step. She would have to come to him, and, even then he didn't know what the connection would bring.

His pulse was beating faster—he could feel the faint throbbing, as he could feel the slender thread of sweat trickling down his back. A faint trembling ran though his hands. He felt like he was sixteen again.

This was nuts, he told himself, absolutely nuts. He was a grown man with a wife at home. A wife who needed him. A sick wife who needed him. A wife with cancer who needed him. And yet, and yet...

He had needs, too, he reminded himself. Needs that he could never seem to put behind him. Davis Wells bit his lip as he struggled to get a grip on himself.

For a second, he thought of his son. His son who was who-knew-where. Davis had tried so hard, and so had Ellen, but, in the end, somehow they'd fallen short, or fate had turned against them.

A thousand times he'd thought about it—was it somehow his fault, or hers? Or was it purely some chemical imbalance in the son they'd raised and loved. That's what his doctor and the counselor had both suggested. But Davis didn't know; that was one thing he'd never made up his mind about.

He was still trying to make up his mind when she pushed away from the tree and moved smoothly forward. Without thinking, he opened his arms and she stepped inside them.

She was soft and warm against his chest and he held her there, firmly, but not so tightly as to squeeze the breath out of her. Then she lifted her face and pressed her lips against his. For a heartbeat, he hesitated. Then his mind shifted into a zone he hadn't entered in a very long time and a great wave of emotions washed across his mind. Lost in the eddies and swirls, he didn't think about the fentanyl crisis, or Lawton Turner, or heading for Kansas. He didn't even think of Ellen.

A car door slammed and headlights flashed on and Davis could feel the tide of emotions began to turn. His mind broke through the surface and he knew where he was and what he was doing. He whispered, "I want you."

"I want you, too."

"Only not here."

"No," she shook her head and he could feel her hair brush against his face. "Not here, and not now."

Tanya lifted her face again so that a shaft of starlight caressed her check. Davis pulled her close. Her breath was warm, her lips were soft. He kissed her again, then pulled back a few inches to study her face at close range. He watched as her eyes slowly opened, reflecting a faint glimmer of light. Shadows lay softly in the curve of her checks and her full lips seemed to call his name. He wanted her more than he had wanted any woman in a long time. And yet something seemed off, wrong. Wrong and sad and rotten to the core, and yet...

Voices drifted through the darkness, mumbled, indistinct, steadily growing closer. Then Davis could hear the crunch of footsteps in the gravel. The woman heard it, too. He could see the lights in her eyes shift toward the sound. She brushed her lips across his.

"I'd better go, but can't we meet in a better place? Somewhere private."

He could hear the smile in her voice and felt the smile on his face. "Can you get away tomorrow night? Say out of town?"

"Yes."

He felt his mind shifting again and he spoke against the movement. "Good. Then I'll get us a room somewhere and we can meet without so many prying eyes and listening ears." He felt as though he needed to apologize, although he wasn't sure why. "I've got to be cautious, you understand?"

She squeezed his hands. "I understand, Davis, I really do."

Tanya let go of his hands. "Now, walk me to my car. Then maybe you better give me ten minutes to get gone before you pull out. No need giving anyone any ammunition, is there?"

"Nope. Let's walk."

Their footsteps reverberated in his ears as they worked their way between vehicles. They sounded loud to him, so loud it seemed as if surely someone would hear them and take notice. A rock seemed to have become lodged in his stomach and the palms of his hands were sweaty. Damn, he was as bad as schoolboy. Davis wiped his palms on his pants.

The woman was looking at him with an expression he couldn't quite read. Depending on the way the chancy moonlight struck her face, she either pitied him or was worried about him. Neither look made any sense to him.

A bird whirled through the darkness in front of them. Hunting, probably, he thought. Lots of creatures hunted at night. Some men, too, he said to himself and smiled.

Lost in thought, he almost barreled into the woman. She had stopped at what he figured was her car, a nondescript, dark colored Chevy. She turned her face up to his.

"Guess I'd better go, Davis. It's getting late and you have to work tomorrow."

"I'm a big boy. I'll be fine." He grinned at her and when she smiled back, he wanted her more than he had wanted anybody in a very, very long time. He reached out in the darkness and pulled her to him, not caring who saw or what they thought. Without thinking, he pressed his lips against hers and felt himself grow hard against her body.

Too quickly for him, the woman broke the kiss, leaning back against her car, gasping for air, then saying "Wow, baby, wow. You do get worked up, don't you?"

Davis took a deep breath and forced his face toward the road. A car was rolling by, headed east, and he watched it as he struggled to get his emotions under control. He'd been stupid. Maybe he'd gotten away with it once, but he couldn't keep on pressing his luck, no matter how strong his desires. He let out the air he'd been holding and turned back to face the woman.

He leaned forward until his face was so close to hers he could feel the warmth of her breath against his skin. "Guess I did tonight."

He brushed his lips across her cheek, then pulled the car door open. "You'd better get rolling before I get worked up again, Tanya."

She slid in behind the wheel and smiled up at him. "Tomorrow, baby."

"I'll call you."

She blew him a kiss, then pressed the starter button. He stepped back and watched her pull away, regretting, at least to some degree, that he hadn't gotten his emotions under control. His eyes followed her taillights as they left the parking lot, tracking them until they were swallowed up by the Missouri night.

He stood there for some time, trying to get a handle on his life—between the fentanyl and Ellen's cancer and now this strange, new, exciting woman, he felt as though he no longer controlled his destiny. Would he go through with what he'd just proposed? Doubt was already creeping through his mind. Wanting a woman was one thing; cheating on Ellen was another. His mind seemed to be whirling in a dozen different directions all at once. He didn't know. He purely didn't know.

Davis Wells shook his head, spun on his heel, and started walking toward his truck. He wondered how much he would sleep this night.

Fifty-five

Memories ran deep through the shadows under the trees lining the sagging barbed wire fence that marked the boundary of the Monroe place. He'd brought Debbie Bonham here after the senior prom. Daylight had been a legitimate promise when they'd finally pulled out. Neither one of them had been the same person they'd been when the night was young. Without question, it had been a night to remember. And now he was back. Only the times and circumstances were both different, very different. On that long ago night, he'd been a young man with dreams and a lifetime of tomorrows; now he was over forty, out of dreams, with tomorrow as uncertain as the hereafter.

Tonight was his, though, and he aimed to make the best of it. If all the cards fell his way, he'd at least pay back Davis Wells for what he'd done to him. Pay him back in spades—first, he'd hold a gun on the sheriff and make the man grovel and sweat. Then, he'd put the business end of the revolver to Wells' head and force him to watch his wife die. Finally, he'd show the bastard more mercy than the prick had ever shown him and put him out of his misery with a bullet to the brain. Then he'd...

Actually, Lawton hadn't thought beyond the killing moment. If his luck were in, he'd be out of state before anybody even knew the sheriff and his wife were dead. Sure, a deputy or two might suspect him, but they'd have to prove he was the killer, and that would take some doing. He'd lose his gun and Tanya's so there'd be nothing to tie him to the crime. Not to mention, Lawton planned to put one hell of a lot of miles between himself and Pratt County before daylight.

The way he had it figured, he and Tanya would split up—just in case anybody had seen them together and started putting two and two together—then reconnect down at his Uncle Forrest's place in Texas in a month or so. Might even slip across the border if things got hot, although there were some damn bad hombres down there these days. Still, hard times forced hard decisions, as Dink Winslow used to say.

Dink had been his cellmate for almost a year—a standup guy who kept his mouth shut and had never once tried to put anything over on him. Old Dink wasn't near as dumb as he let on, either. A sudden urge to see Dink swept over Lawton and he smiled in the soft Missouri night. Dink would be good backup, and it never hurt to have backup. However, that wasn't happening, and Lawton had years ago learned to deal with reality.

Lawton could feel his nerves starting to tingle. Midnight was sneaking around the corner. Tanya should be along any minute and then they'd get started.

They'd leave the vehicles here—the old dirt road that led to the rotting skeleton of an abandoned tobacco barn was off the main road a good twenty yards, set back in a cutaway that had been there for as long as Lawton could remember. He had no idea why someone had carved it out of the landscape decades before, but a line of trees had grown up along the fence row that fronted it and weeds and wildflowers had partially reclaimed the land, so that at night the spot was rendered nearly black, dark enough so no one would notice it from the road.

The only danger was crossing the road, but chance was always a factor. Traffic was usually light on the road, especially at night, certainly after midnight.

Once they crossed the road, they'd work their way across the field that lay on the west side of the house—it had been mowed a couple of weeks before and the going wouldn't be bad, especially as the moon was full tonight—then come up through what had once been a garden and circle around behind the house.

Next, they'd grab the wife and haul her out to the old building that looked like it might have been a garage back in the 50s. From there, they'd have a clear view of the sheriff's arrival and be ready the second he stepped into the cone of light cast by the big security light.

Then the fun would begin.

Lawton peered at his watch again. 12:07. Time to roll. Where was Tanya?

Lawton eased the door open and stepped out into the night, closing the door softly behind him. For the final time, he checked his gun, wishing he could risk a smoke, before deciding against it, then walked around to the front of the truck and leaned against its still warm body.

Butterflies fluttered in his stomach and he wiped the palms of his hands on the legs of his trousers. Wouldn't be long now. Only a few more minutes and he'd pay the debt he owed. His mother had always preached "Lawton, pay your debts." Well, this was one debt Lawton Turner sure as hell aimed to pay.

He peered east into the darkness, his eyes searching for headlights, his heart starting to hammer a touch harder in his chest. Davis Wells was supposed to be one tough man. Lawton grinned—he and the sheriff would both find out how tough they really were long before the sun rose again.

Fifty-six

Ellen slipped serenely out of a memory. She been remembering her sixteenth birthday when her mom had baked her an angel food cake, slathered it with pink icing. At lunchtime, Ellen and her mom, dad, and best friend Eva Mae had walked down to the stock pond for her birthday celebration. Her mother had packed a picnic basket filled with ham sandwiches, apple slices and cheese, and walnuts they had hulled back during the winter. The early July afternoon sunlight had been soft and warm and they had spread a blanket under one of the willows and unpacked the basket. Birds had been singing in the trees and a gentle breeze had carried the scent of new mown hay to them. Everyone had been smiling and happy. Then her mind shifted and the memory faded like a person disappearing in a sudden, heavy fog.

She'd been so deep into her memory that, for a moment, Ellen simply sat in the old rocker in the kitchen, eyes wide open, her mind swirling, trying to recapture the past. Then the mantle clock started chiming and she was back in the alive night. Ellen rose smoothly from the rocker, alert, listening, wondering.

She stood silently, the linoleum smooth against her bare feet, trying to decide what she wanted to do. She considered fixing another cup of tea and reading the new James Lee Burke novel. Then she thought about seeing if there was a good, old movie playing on the television. But the longer she stood there, the stronger she felt herself growing, until she finally decided to get dressed and take a short walk in the moonlight that was painting the yard.

She felt good, all right, but not quite up to traipsing down the front steps at night. Instead, she headed for the kitchen door. Halfway to the back porch, she remembered Davis telling her about his informant. The man didn't sound over dangerous, but Ellen knew she'd feel more comfortable if she had a gun.

She swung around and walked to what had once been the sitting room, where she lifted the revolver out of the drawer. Ellen checked to make sure it was loaded, jammed it between her jeans and top, then resumed her march toward the moonlight.

Her muscles felt strong tonight and her mind seemed as clear as when she had been in school. Ellen wondered if her cancer were in remission. She wondered for only a handful of heartbeats because hope was a chancy thing—it kept you going at times when by all rights you should have given up, yet there was a danger to it, as well. Hoping against reality only caused heartache and another small death. Ellen wasn't sure how many more of those she could handle.

Fifty-seven

One lousy cigarette of mediocre weed wasn't going to get him through the night. Birdman could feel his nerves working like a colony of worms on speed and his skull felt like it was an overripe cantaloupe starting to crack. He'd tried to sleep, but that had been only an exercise in futility—another in a long line.

Twenty minutes ago, the walls of the old garage had started to close in on him and he'd gotten to his feet and strolled outside. Judging by the moon, midnight was either just coming or going and Birdman wondered how he was possibly going to get through the rest of the night.

When he'd been a kid, his mother had taken him and his siblings to church from time to time. Mostly they went to the Methodist Church on Bethel Pike, because it was less than a mile from their house. One of the songs the Methodists had liked to sing was "Leaning on the Everlasting Arms." Years later, one night when sleep wouldn't come, he'd thought of the song and somehow the title had gotten mingled with the long hours between dusk and daylight until Birdman had come to automatically call them the everlasting hours. Now, it seemed like he'd get to enjoy a few more of them.

In the canopy of the trees growing behind the old garage, birds stirred restlessly and from a nearby field came the yappings of a coyote. Coyotes had started moving into Pratt County a dozen years ago and now they seemed to be everywhere. Birdman had even seen them in town. Back in the early spring, he'd seen one trotting across the courthouse lawn.

Coyotes made him think of dogs—weird, killer dogs—and Birdman had always been sorta afraid of dogs, and he was sure enough afraid of coyotes. Coyotes killed rabbits and birds and smaller dogs, and he was always afraid a pack of them was going to come after him. He didn't like their looks or the way they acted. You could never tell where they would go or what they would do, sort of like Lawton Turner. Maybe Lawton Turner could be called a human coyote? Whatever you called him, simply thinking of Lawton Turner made Birdman nervous and he pushed off the ground and started drifting toward the house. Even though he couldn't go inside, simply being close to the sheriff's house made him feel a touch safer. Damn, but his head was cracking.

Fifty-eight

The headlights probed the darkness as she wheeled onto Highway H. Before the woman, the road unfurled, white in the moonlight. She had her window down and could hear the rush of the slipstream and, once, the screech of a bird, a hawk, she thought. Odors drifted on the night air: fresh manure, along with the scents of fertilizer and animal hides mingling with the smell water makes as it strikes the ground— somebody had irrigated a field recently.

Tanya was nervous now. Tremors were sluicing through her body and her fingers were fidgety on the wheel. She risked a glance at the dashboard clock. Damn, she was a good ten minutes late, maybe fifteen. She'd driven the road before on a test run, but only in the daylight. Everything seemed so different at night. Plus, the going was slower. She had to be careful, especially on the curves. Of all nights, this was the one where she truly couldn't afford to wreck. If the crash didn't kill her, Lawton would. This night was so important to him; nothing must be allowed to go wrong. Tanya glanced at the clock again, bit her lower lip, and pressed down on the accelerator. A straight stretch of highway lay before her and she had to make up time. Lawton was going to be so pissed.

Fifty-nine

This was one of those nights Davis regretted he'd given up smoking. The urge to smoke always happened when the stress load got too heavy, and heaven knows he was under a shit-ton of stress. Between Ellen's cancer and the damn fentanyl deaths, plus the woman with the slender face and long black hair, he was under so much stress he could feel it throbbing in his temples. A cigarette would surely have helped, or even one of his dad's Dutch Masters, but he'd given up nicotine twenty years ago and he was too damn old to pick up the habit again.

Davis looked back at the bar—he could also use another drink. But alcohol was one more thing he didn't need. Ellen might smell it on his breath and even though he could explain it so she would accept it, the whole process would take forever. Plus, it would add to his stress. Not to mention that his wife didn't need anything else to worry about.

Which was fine, because he had enough to worry about for both of them. Forget about his personal life for a minute—the job by itself was plenty. Especially with all the recent drug deaths. Starting with Mark Chisholm, Davis went over them in his mind, one by one, in the order of their passing, trying to find some common thread other than the fentanyl-laced heroin. He went through the list three times, giving himself a headache in the process, always coming back to the same point, the point that twisted in his gut like electrified barbed-wire— every one of the victims had some connection to him.

He'd been Mark's baseball coach, Eddie Dillard had been in the Optimist Club with him, Betty Werner was a second cousin on his mother's side—the list went on and on. Some he knew personally and some he knew their parents, but one way and another, they all circled back to him. And while Davis knew he wasn't the most beloved man in Pratt County, the only person he could think of who hated him enough to kill an innocent person so he would suffer was Lawton Turner. He wished he'd put out the APB sooner.

Davis kicked at a patch of gravel and started walking toward his vehicle. Moving felt better and he picked up the pace. A minute later, he popped the door and climbed into the cab. He fired the engine up and checked the time. Midnight had come and gone. Willie had the night shift and wasn't likely to be busy. Checking in wouldn't hurt. Davis tugged his cell phone out of its holster and punched in Willie's number.

"Boss, what's up?"

"Not much, Willie. Just thought I'd check in with you before I called it a night."

"Keeping late hours, aren't you?"

"You know how it is."

"Sure do." Willie paused, as if to give Davis a chance to say what was on his mind. When only silence filled the gap, he cleared his throat and said, "Everything's quiet here except for a fistfight outside the Dairy Queen. Oh, and Ted and Mary Simpson getting into another shouting match."

"Any word on Lawton Turner?"

"Nothing substantial. I've made calls to some of my informers, the ones I think shoot straight with me, at least most of the time, and nobody knows much. Eddie Fitzgerald said he did see him earlier in the week driving out near Croley Bend in a Jeep, and the younger Lassiter kid said he'd talked to him day before yesterday on the phone.

Wouldn't say what they talked about, which means it wasn't anything good. But at least we've confirmed what we figured, Lawton Turner is somewhere here in Pratt County, or at least he was. Maybe he's moved on."

"Don't think so. My gut's telling me he came back for a reason and it's not a reason that's good for anybody but him. Until we figure out what brought him back, or find him, we'd better assume that badass is out there somewhere."

"Expect you're right. Been getting bad vibes all day. You know he's supposed to have a real problem with you."

Davis rubbed at his eyes. It was late, especially for a middle-aged sheriff. "Yeah, I've heard. But what am I supposed to do about that?"

"Don't have any answers for you, boss, but you know what they say?"

"No, Willie, I don't. What do they say?"

"The words that keep running through my brain are from that old Charley Pride song, something about snakes crawling at night. And if a man was ever a snake, well that man is Lawton Turner."

Davis started to laugh, but he choked it down. Not that he was particularly superstitious, but tempting fate had never seemed like a good move to him. "Hear that. But I'm gonna shut 'er down and head for the house. I'll keep my eyes open."

Willie laughed. "Better make that wide open, boss."

Davis laughed and disconnected. As he pulled out of the parking lot, he had the sudden sense he was missing an important factor in the equation. All the way to the turnoff it worried him like a boil on his butt.

Sixty

One minute he'd been drifting, his mind flowing free, as though pushed by a steady wind, thinking about his childhood: the rope swing hanging from a limb in the gum tree that rose out of the back yard, towering over the shed and the chicken coop, the way his mother's fried potatoes had smelled, his friend Jimmy Bates, and Linda McEver. All gone now, except in his mind, or what passed for his mind these days.

The next minute he was back on the sheriff's land, the moon shining so bright Birdman thought he might be able to read a newspaper by the moonlight, and somebody moving under the grape arbor that covered the space between the porch and the root cellar.

The hairs on the back of his neck prickled and he felt a nerve jump in his left check as he stepped deeper into the shadows. He was behind the house, off to the east maybe thirty yards, deep in the cluster of locust trees that had grown up between the garage and the field behind it. Birdman felt safer in the shadows. Nighttime always had its advantages, and over the years he'd made good use of them. Tonight, though, felt different. Maybe it was being halfway straight, or maybe some long hidden animal instinct was trying to warn him, or perhaps it was simply that his brain had slipped another notch. In any case, fear was racing through him like a rogue electrical current.

Birdman wondered if the person moving out there in the dark was Lawton Turner. He was getting ready to ease deeper into the trees when a woman stepped out into the moonlight.

Birdman didn't recognize her, but, after watching her move smoothly down the stepping-stone path to the picket fence, he figured she must be the sheriff's wife. She was too confident, too much at ease to be an intruder. Now what the woman was doing walking around her yard in the middle of the night was more than Birdman could figure out.

He eased back to the front of the trees and took a long look in the direction the woman was walking. If his memory were to be trusted, always a doubtful plan, if she kept walking along the same line, she would be heading toward the old barn at the bottom of the swale. Why the sheriff's wife would want to pay a visit to the barn this time of night was truly a mystery. However, since the cover appeared good and the shadows deep in that direction, Birdman thought he just might slip along behind her and see what was going on. That should take his mind off his needs—well, it might help some.

Birdman watched as the woman opened the gate in the picket fence, then walked across the place where the sheriff parked his truck. When she was about twenty yards beyond his vantage point, Birdman eased out of the tree line and began following her, taking care to stay in the shadows, using first the garage, then a few of the raggedy cherry trees for cover. Now and then, he could hear his footsteps rustling through the grass and once he stepped on a fallen tree branch. The crack of rotten wood drew him up short, but the woman seemed not to notice as she walked steadily down the slope, stepping fluidly in and out of the moonlight.

Sixty-one

He waited until the headlights swung into the narrow cutoff before he stepped out of the tree line. He could make out the silhouette of her face, shimmering faintly in the dashboard lights, and he hustled down the bank as she cut the motor.

She was sliding out of the car when he grabbed the door handle and jerked it open. For a heartbeat, her face was crinkled in fear. Then he stepped into the shaft of light falling through the open door and the woman smiled.

"Lawton."

He grasped her outstretched hand and helped her out of the car. "How did it go?"

"What? Oh, with the sheriff? It went fine. He got a little worked up, but I got him calmed down. I'm guessing he's about fifteen minutes behind me."

"Then we've got to be moving. You've got your pistol, I presume?"

She patted the left front pocket of her jeans. "Right here."

"And it's loaded?"

"Sure. Well, I guess it is."

"Make sure, Tanya. We can't afford any slipups, not tonight."

She pulled the gun out of her pocket and held it so that the interior lights reflected off the barrel. The clip was in and she smiled. She'd never seen Lawton so tense—it wouldn't do to upset him tonight.

"It's loaded."

"All right, then, come on. We need to get moving, like now. I want to be in place long before the bastard shows up."

Tanya felt a trembling run through her legs, but she mouthed a soft "Yes." Lawton was already turning, so she eased the door shut and hurried after him. At the edge of the road, he looked both ways, then jogged across. She ran after him, stumbling once, but catching herself and hurrying on.

Across the road, he paused to survey the landscape, then jumped over a shallow ditch and stepped over barbed wire leaning south. Tanya followed, making a mess of the jump, catching a shoe in the barbed wire, then falling forward, hitting the ground hard, making way too much noise, knocking the breath out of her diaphragm.

She lay there a moment, gasping for air, knowing Lawton was going to be furious. She closed her eyes—she couldn't bear to see how angry he was. She felt hands grab her arms and then she was being pulled to her feet. Tanya opened her eyes, but kept them lowered as she brushed herself off.

"Damn, woman, what the fuck do you think you're doing?" he asked in a low, hoarse whisper. "I told you twice how we had to be quiet and the first damn thing you do is fall down and make enough noise to wake up half Pratt County."

Hot tears filled her eyes and she sobbed softly. "I'm sorry, Lawton."

He shook her. Shook her so hard she thought she might be coming apart. "Crying's not going to help a damn thing, Tanya, so get a grip and let's get moving. If you can't do that, then get your sorry ass back to your car, get in it, and start driving. And I don't care where to. I've never asked you for a damn thing, and now when I do you can't even stay on your feet."

He let go of her then, stepping back, starting to turn away. Moonlight highlighted his face and she could read the anger etched there. "Well, what's it gonna be?"

Tanya swiped at her tears, sniffled. Then she shook her head so the hair whirled out from her skull. In her imagination it flowed like a moving swirl of dark water. She bit her lip and straightened until she stood as tall as she could. "I'm coming, Lawton, I'm coming with you."

"All right, then. Let's roll. Just follow me and, for damn sure, don't fall down again. We're going to swing around to the left so we come up behind the house. There's a tall hedge of some sort angled off north from the kitchen. We'll come around through there and be in the house before Wells' wife has the first clue. Once we grab her, we'll slide back outside and wait for him. Just follow my lead. You got that, Tanya?"

"I've got it. I'll be there for you, baby."

Her emotions were flowing so strong right then she didn't know how she could hold them. She hoped he would kiss her, at least give her a hug. But all he did was whirl around and start working his way through the field, weeds and grasses parting as he passed. She brushed her hands against each other, then started after him, picking her way with care, patting her jeans to make sure she still had the pistol.

Sixty-two

The breeze was gentle against her face and the moonlight was so bright she didn't need a flashlight in the open places. She crossed the patch of grass that fronted the gate to the old barnyard and leaned against the rail fence. When she and Davis had first moved to the farm, they had talked about raising hogs and sheep and chickens. They had also talked about raising children. Well, they had raised one child, a son. And, though they had done their honest best, that hadn't gone the way they had planned. In fact, she thought as she stared across the empty barnyard, nothing had gone as they planned, at least not for a long time, not since their son had slipped away from them and the cancer had slipped into her body.

She shook her head in an effort to dislodge the dark thoughts, then glanced at the moon. It had drifted since she started her stroll and she guessed she had, too. Why had she walked down to the old barn? She rarely walked at night, and when she did, it was usually no more than a brief stroll around the yard. Since her treatments, she had never walked so far, certainly not by herself. Perhaps it was because she felt different tonight—stronger yes, but something else, too, something she couldn't quite put her finger on.

Ellen studied the moon; it was large tonight, soft silver in color and slightly misshapen, as though the sky were pressing against it from all sides. She smiled. Pressure from all sides—now that was a feeling she knew.

She turned away from the barn and started back up the slope, feeling the blood flowing through her veins, her head clear for the first time in months, and her heart beating strongly. Tonight, she'd surprise Davis, and in a good way.

Ellen tried to remember what time she had left the house. For sure, it had been late. He should be home any minute. Her lips curved into a smile and she started walking faster, allowing herself to hope, at least for a few strides, that life could be, would be, good again.

Sixty-three

Birdman stepped quickly behind the tree he'd been leaning against. The woman's sudden turn had caught him by surprise. One minute she'd been leaning against the fence looking up at the moon as though she planned to gaze for hours, the next she'd pivoted and started marching back up the slope as though her ass were on fire. Hell, he'd understood the woman was sick—cancer, or something. What the hell was going on?

His right eye twitched and his stomach sorta turned over; a wave of weakness shot through him. He wasn't up to any sudden moves or surprises, not in the shape he was in. If he were high or really mellow, well things would be different. But hell, a few drags off some lousy weed flat out didn't cut it.

The woman had passed him, moving toward the house at a pace Birdman didn't think he could match. The wind was kicking up—he could hear it rustling the leaves and he figured he could start following the woman again. Simply having her in sight made him feel better. Tonight, he didn't want to be alone, certainly not down by the old barn.

He wasn't even sure if he could stand the garage again by his lonesome. Something was going to happen—he could sense it, out in the night, looming, gathering force. Something was going to happen tonight, and he could feel in his bones that it wasn't going to be good for the old Birdman.

He began to ease away from the trees, moving closer to the fence that separated the dying orchard from the field. He shot a quick glance over the fence. It wouldn't do to have someone slipping in on his backside. A vision of Lawton Turner's face flashed across his mind and he shivered. Birdman knew, and would freely admit, that he known some real hardasses in his life, but the one he feared most was Lawton Turner.

The woman was nearly at the garage. Birdman halted until she walked by the old building and across the patch of gravel where the sheriff parked his vehicle. Just as she swung open the gate to the yard, the sound of another footfall reached his ears. Instantly he crouched and began covering ground in a jog. Just liked he'd sensed—something was happening. He had no clue what, but his nerves were singing, which was never a good sign.

He slipped around the garage and by a rusty mowing machine, stumbled over the stump of a tree that had been cut down years before, windmilling forward but staying upright, heading for what the sheriff had called the old smokehouse. Once he reached the shadows of the building, he caught his breath, then curled around the back and ran hard for the bushes that edged the east side of the yard.

Under those bushes it was dark, and Birdman sprawled flat on his stomach, slithering forward until he could clearly see the rear crown of the root cellar, the back porch, the light burning in the kitchen, and a slice of the west side yard.

Birdman took a cautious look back toward the east side yard and the fence that separated the yard from the drive. The woman was nowhere to be seen. Then, out of the corner of his right eye, he glimpsed her curling around the corner of the front of the house. Seconds later, he heard her footsteps on the front porch steps.

Something, or somebody, was moving down by the garden. Bushes crackled as whatever it was moved. He twisted his head toward the sound, peering through the darkness. At first, he couldn't see anything. He held his breath and closed his eyes, focusing all his attention on sound. Listening carefully, being aware of strange sounds—sounds that didn't belong, had kept his sorry ass out of bad trouble many a time.

Nothing. Birdman started counting. He had reached seven when a bird twittered and something small moved close by, ruffling the leaves of a bush only a couple of feet to his right. Then, so softly that he wondered if it was only his imagination, Birdman heard a whisper. He squeezed his eyes more tightly shut, listening even more intently. Just at the edge of sound, another voice, a woman's this time. Birdman opened his eyes and inched out of the bushes.

The voices had come from the west side of the house. What in the hell was anybody doing over there? That was way weird—had to be trouble. Maybe kids out farting around, or druggies looking for a place to rob. That he could understand, to a degree, but the sheriff's house was way the hell out in the middle of nowhere. Which was okay as far as not having any nosy neighbors, but it was a damn long way for an addict to come for what might be a meager haul. Besides, even a drughead ought to know better than to hit the fudging sheriff's house.

The voices spoke again, louder than before, and Birdman shifted his eyes a few yards to the right, honing in on the sound, wondering. Then a figure stepped out of a patch of milkweed into pool of moonlight and Birdman had to fight hard to keep from shitting all over himself.

Sixty-four

Davis pressed down harder on the brake as he passed Art Dexter's house. Just ahead was a tricky passage—the road did a double S as it went down Butler Hill, then swirled back up out of the bottom and climbed to the top of the ridge that ran all the way to the county line. He wished he could tap the brake on his nerves; they were making his guts churn.

That was the trouble with wanting something you shouldn't have. Although he still didn't see how it was fair that he was supposed to do without sex for the rest of his life, and him a healthy, virile man with a strong sexual drive, Davis acknowledged it still was wrong to be unfaithful to his wife.

Until Ellen had gotten sick, he'd never thought about another woman, not seriously anyway. Oh, he'd taken a second look at a few. But hell, all his life he'd heard that just because you bet on one horse didn't mean you couldn't watch the race. Anyway, before her cancer he never seriously considered having an affair. Oh, he'd fantasized occasionally, but every man did that.

No, this was something more; Tanya was something more. And she'd come into his life so suddenly and when he was at such a vulnerable juncture that the want in him was rising like the Missouri in flood stage. No way did he want to do Ellen wrong, but he wasn't one hundred percent certain he could hold out forever. Already, he'd noticed the way he looked in the morning mirror. He hadn't been sleeping good and his appetite had been off. Not to mention that he'd been drinking more than he should have. These days, his skin had a grayish pallor and new lines seemed to etch his face every day. Speaking of drinking—he'd have to have a double when he got home.

Thinking of home made him worry about Ellen and a wave of guilt washed through him, leaving him feeling dirty and ashamed. He should have been home with her tonight and not meeting up with the dark-haired woman with the soft, warm lips. Acting like that made him a jerk, an asshole, a son-of-a-bitch, and if there was anything to the karma he kept hearing about, he was going to have to pay.

As the truck came out of the final curve, Davis muttered a few choice words and pressed down on the accelerator. He'd straighten up, that's what he'd do. That's what he had to do.

He acknowledged he'd told himself that same story a dozen times before. Not for the first time, he wondered what would happen if the shit hit the fan. Maybe Ellen would understand, maybe. Or perhaps she could find a way to forgive him. In her own way, she was a damn strong woman, a damn special woman. That he'd known all along. It was one of the reasons he'd asked her to marry him. And then, first with their son drifting away, followed by the cancer coming on, well she'd surely been tested. Yet she was still standing.

Well, so was he. But he wasn't betting the home place on how long he could hold out. Sainthood wasn't in his future and any man could only stand so much. Willpower was all right, but life could rear up ugly sometimes. And every man had needs. Davis recognized he had needs. He surely had needs.

The truck crested the ridge, rolling out of the darkness into the moon-splattered night. Davis glanced out the passenger window— he was going by the old Gleason farm. Don Gleason had gone to school with him, played basketball with him, gone on a camping trip to the Ozarks with him. Then, one hot July day two years ago, Don had slipped his dad's double-barreled twelve gauge out of the house, strolled down behind the barn, put the business end of the barrel in his mouth and pulled the trigger. As far as Davis knew, no one had ever figured out why Don had blown his brains out. Law enforcement had taught him there was always a reason behind any action. Finding out what that reason was, well, that was another matter.

A deer stood in the field, its head lifted, nose pointed toward the road. It stood alone in the moonlight, as still as though it had been carved from granite. Maybe, Davis thought, if things fell out the wrong way, he'd be that alone someday. He wondered how he would feel, and what he would do. He was so damn confused; he just wasn't sure about anything anymore. Not about the drug deaths, or Tanya, or Ellen, or even himself. He felt so alone that part of him wanted to cry. Only real men didn't cry and, besides, crying never solved anything. Davis reached over and cranked the radio up. Then he put the hammer down, racing the moonbeams, his fears, and the demons whirling inside his brain.

Sixty-five

"What the hell?" Lawton Turner took another step into the yard, peering through the darkness, trying to find a way to see around the bushes that grew just outside the kitchen window. In the kitchen a light burned; he could see the stove, the kitchen table, and the refrigerator. Lawton eased a step to his right. Hell, the whole house was lit up like a fudging Christmas tree.

That wasn't supposed to have happened. It was well past midnight and the woman was supposed to be sick, dying with some crazy cancer. What was she doing with every freaking light in the house on?

Lawton studied the house more closely. Well, maybe every light wasn't on, but several were and now Lawton wasn't sure what to do. Hell, he wasn't one bit confident the woman was even in the house. Maybe she'd gone out for a midnight stroll. Or maybe Davis Wells had snuck in on his blind side. The way his luck had been running, that would just about be par for the course.

Crouching low, Lawton duckwalked toward the house, angling north so he could get a good look at the driveway. If the asshole had slipped in on him, there was still plenty of time to retreat. He could always try again another night, although he was getting worried about

Tanya. Her nerves seemed to be ramping up, and for sure she was getting on his last few. Should have known better than to bring her along. He'd never worked well with a partner—they always seemed to let him down. Granted, there were situations where an extra man or gun came in handy, and Tanya had been essential for the setup he'd planned. But maybe he should have forgotten her and gone to Plan B, whatever the hell that might have been.

Lawton sighed—too late to worry about that now. He worked around a birdbath and a stump of a tree that had been one big mother in its time. Then he caught a glimpse of the security light. Another step and he could see the last thirty yards of the drive and the place where the sheriff always parked—both were empty. Maybe his luck was still in; maybe he could still pull this off.

Twisting around, he looked off toward the weed-choked garden. All he could see were weeds and shadows slow dancing in the rising breeze. Then, as he started to head back to look for her, he caught a glimpse of Tanya's face, naked and frightened in the moonfall. He waved her toward him with his hands.

"What is it, Lawton?" the woman murmured.

"Damn it, Tanya, keep it down. Your loud mouth is going to get us killed."

"Sorry."

"Not as sorry as you're going to be if you don't keep quiet. We're trying to surprise them, not rouse up the neighbors. Understand?"

"Yes, yes, and I'm sorry. What do you want me to do?" She reached out a hand and touched his right arm. He shook her hand off.

"Just be still a minute and listen. Thought I heard something."

"Where?"

"Out there—on the other side of the drive. Now shut the fuck up and listen."

Lawton turned his eyes back toward the security light. He was sure he'd heard something out there in the dark on the far side of the pool of light. Only he didn't know for sure what he'd heard. It had sounded like somebody moving in the dark. But it could have a dog or a cat, maybe even a coyote. Only the night before, he'd seen one across the road from the cabin. He'd be glad to see the country go back to the coyotes and foxes and wolves. People were the ruination of so much. Times had been better when he'd been a kid. Sure, his folks had been poor, but they'd lived off by themselves and hadn't had to answer to anybody, let alone take shit off a prick of a sheriff.

He let his eyes drift along the drive, then shifted his line of sight out to the edge of the pool of light. His eyes were adjusting to the darkness and he could make out a couple of scraggly trees, a shed with a bad case of the leans, even the body of an old car. But he couldn't see anybody, or any animal. He took a deep breath and readied himself to move closer to the house.

"Lawton?"

Her voice was so soft he thought for a second he was imagining things. He inclined his head toward her and spoke softly out of the right corner of his mouth. "What?"

"Think I hear something."

"What?"

"A woman's voice. Sounds like she's singing."

"Maybe it's the radio."

"No, don't think so. Listen."

Lawton closed his eyes, held his breath. All he could hear was the wind worrying the branches of the trees beside the picket fence. Then he heard a faint sound. The wind had fallen off and the sound was clear, like a distant church bell on Sunday morning. Tanya had been right. It was a woman singing. Sounded like she was singing a hymn. He recognized the tune, though he couldn't name it. His mother had sung it, sung it all those years ago when he had been a kid. A lifetime ago.

Opening his eyes, he peered out toward the fence and the graveled drive beyond. All he could see were a few shadows tap dancing in the breeze that had started to rise again. He checked left, then right—still nothing. Lawton cocked his head and listened, hard.

The only sound was the wind. Then he heard the voice again. Coming from the front of the house, he thought. Lawton took a step in that direction, then another. The wind rose suddenly, then fell off again and he heard the singing clearly this time, unmistakably coming from the front of the house.

Another sound drifted out of the darkness and he turned to look beyond the fence, closer to the outline of the building he could barely make out. Something, or someone, had moved out there. Lawton studied Tanya, trying to decide if he could trust her to bring the woman to him. He had bad vibes about what was out there wandering around in the dark, and he'd learned long ago to trust his instincts. Still, the first step in his plan was to find the sheriff's wife and get her under control. Lawton took a final look toward the picket fence, then motioned to Tanya as he started moving, going low, staying in the shadows when he could, trying to step carefully, doing his best to move when he heard the wind. Now was not the time to fuck up. Lawton hoped the wind would hold this time.

Sixty-six

Birdman couldn't stop his body from shaking. It was shaking so hard he was afraid he was going to shake himself apart. He pushed deeper under the bush. He had no clue what kind it was, but it sure was full of sharp-edged branches. They kept stabbing him in the back and the neck, even poking his face.

Not that he gave a hairy rat's ass. He'd seen who was out there and wanted no part of that scene. If he'd been sure he could make it, Birdman would have jumped up and started running like hell. But he wasn't one bit confident. Lawton Turner was like a two-legged snake, deadly, liable to strike without warning. Birdman scooted deeper into the branches and leaves of the bush, trying to be quiet, desperate to blend in. He took a deep breath, then held it as he closed his eyes.

After a minute, he had to breathe. Plus, it was way too damn nerve wracking not knowing what Lawton Turner was up to. Stuck under the bush, Birdman had no clue what that rattlesnake Turner was doing, and he had to know. His life depended on it, of that he was sure. He sucked in air and forced his body forward, opening his eyes, pressing his face against the outside leaves of the bush, peering across the yard.

There Turner was, and a woman with him. What the hell was going on?

Birdman felt his guts curdle again. He should be getting the hell out of there. And he would—as soon as he could move without taking too much of a chance that Lawton Turner would see him. But first he needed to get a better handle on what Turner was doing. Birdman bit his lower lip, forced himself to look again.

Turner and the woman were creeping along the west side of the house, heading for the front porch. Why were they doing that?

Birdman wished he had some speed. Maybe his mind would shift into gear. He looked off toward the drive. Where was the damn sheriff? The law was always around when he was trying to make a buy or when he finally got high. But now that he needed them, they might as well of been on the far side of the moon.

Birdman turned back to the west in time to see the woman disappearing around the side of the house. He figured Turner was ahead of her, up to nothing good in the night. Question was, what the fuck was old Birdman going to do? For a long moment, he thought again about making a run for it, but the fear that the minute he was out in the moonlight Lawton Turner would step around the corner made him reconsider.

He eased out of the bush, crouching low, ready to move in any direction at the first sight or sound of Turner or the woman. He couldn't see either of them and the night had gone stone silent. He was getting ready to start easing toward the garage when he remembered the pistol and shotgun he'd seen in the house. He'd never been a gun man, never a violent man, but this was different. Birdman had a real bad feeling he just might die before the night was over.

He couldn't see anybody, and, as far as he knew, the sheriff's wife was still around the front of the house. He eyed the back porch, then the lighted kitchen beyond. Nothing moved. Way he saw it, with Lawton Turner so close he could almost see him, old Birdman's ass was cooked if he wasn't carrying. What choice did he have? This was one time he had to roll the dice. Swallowing hard, he started moving for the back door, going as quickly as he could without making a lot of noise. His guts felt like he'd swallowed two feet of barbed wire, but Birdman kept moving.

Sixty-seven

"Good evening, Mrs. Wells."

Ellen jerked in her chair, fear rushing through her, the hair on her arms standing up. She rose quickly, looking left and right, trying to see who was out there beyond the light.

Whoever it was knew her name, but she didn't recognize the voice. It wouldn't be somebody there to rob her, not using her name. The voice hadn't sounded like any of Davis' deputies. She supposed he could have hired a new one, but surely a deputy would have come up the drive, not gone slipping around the side of the house in the dark.

The voice sounded like it had come from her right. She stepped back into the deeper shadows, shifting her eyes toward the edge of the porch. All she could see was the vague outline of the huge lilacs bush that had been there when they had moved in. Maybe she'd drifted off to sleep and had a flash dream. Some of her medications produced weird side effects. But surely not—the voice had been so clear. She eased a step to her right.

Before she could take another, a man stepped into the moonlight and she remembered Davis had told her he had a witness stashed in the old garage. What was the fool doing out in the yard? Ellen was certain Davis would have told him to stay put. Thinking about Davis' witness made her remember the gun in her pocket and she instantly felt better. Then the man stepped quickly to the edge of the porch. Ellen gasped. The man had a gun in his hand and he was pointing it at her. She could feel her body shaking.

"Who are you?" she croaked. She could hear the trembling in her voice, but she didn't care. Anyway, she didn't see what she could do about it.

"Names don't mean much," the man said as he walked to the steps and started climbing them. The gun in his right hand was very steady. Ellen could see the opening at the end of the barrel —the man was that close. Shadows still darkened most of the man's face, but the part that was visible was unknown to her. This couldn't be Davis' witness; he would never have allowed such a person to have a gun. She thought again about the gun in the right front pocket of her jeans. Decided instantly against trying to get it out. The man on the top step of the porch looked like he meant business.

"What matters," the man said, "is what a man does. And what another man does to him. Your husband did me bad wrong, and tonight he's going to pay and so, unfortunately, are you."

The man stepped up on the porch into a slender slant of moonlight. She could see he was smiling. Only his smile never came close to making it to his eyes. Ellen shivered. She hoped she wouldn't cry.

"Right now, Mrs. Wells, we need you to come down off the porch and walk around to the back of your house. We'll wait for your husband there. I have it on good authority that he'll be home any minute."

The man nodded at the steps. "Come on now, let's go. Understand you've been sick and I don't want to be rough with you, but I will if you make me. Better start walking now. Don't make it worse than it has to be." He motioned toward the steps with the business end of the gun.

As Ellen started for the steps, she noticed the woman for the first time. Standing at the edge of the porch, close to the lilac bush, her face was thin and pale against the darkness.

As she maneuvered down the steps, Ellen glanced at the woman, then turned at the man's direction and started walking toward the back of the house. As she moved, Ellen shot a quick glance toward the road, half-hoping to see headlights. Half-scared they would be turning in at the drive.

The man walked closely behind her, holding the gun pointed at the middle of her back, prodding her with it when she slowed. Ellen fought to hold back tears; they wouldn't help. Crying never did. She kept moving, praying the man or the woman wouldn't search her. If they didn't, she still had a chance. She and Davis would both still have a chance. Since the cancer had come, that was all she ever allowed herself to hope for, a chance. Just one good chance.

~ * ~

She couldn't stop her hands from trembling and her lips wanted to tremble, too. She wanted to cry, but that wouldn't help her, or Davis. For sure it wouldn't make any difference to the man leaning against the fence a couple of feet to her right. And she doubted it would make much difference to the woman who stood to her left. The woman was close; Ellen could smell her perfume and, when the wind fell off, hear her tapping her fingernails on the gun in her left hand.

The woman hadn't spoken and Ellen wondered if she was a mute. She let her eyes drift across the woman's face, then down the drive to the road. She let her eyes drift east along the road, the way Davis would be coming. Where was he? He was hardly ever so late. Maybe he wouldn't be able to make it home tonight. Perhaps he'd run into a bad case. There had been so many deaths lately, all that fentanyl Davis had told her about. No reason to doubt there would be another one. She allowed herself to hope. It was awful to wish for somebody's death, but maybe such a tragedy would, in its own peculiar way, save Davis. Maybe even save her.

Simply considering the possibility of living freed her mind and the question that had been swirling around in the turmoil rose to the surface. Ellen turned to face the man. His body was covered in shadows, but his face was highlighted by a streak of moonlight.

"Who are you?" She was pleased her voice sounded firmer now, more under control.

The man was silent so long she began to think he wasn't going to answer, that perhaps her question had angered him. Then she heard his clothes rustling against the planking as he stepped closer, so close she could smell burning tobacco from the glowing cigarette dangling from his mouth.

He pulled the cigarette out and tossed it into the night. He laughed a little under his breath. "Seeing as how it won't matter even a little bit to you in a few moments, don't guess it will hurt to tell you. In a way, you could argue you have the right to know." He laughed again, quite softly, as though to himself.

"My name is Lawton Turner and I aim to make your husband pay tonight."

"Pay for what?"

"For what? For what? For running me out of the place I grew up in and for taking away almost two years of my life. That's what for, Mrs. Davis Wells. And don't you doubt for one minute I'm going to make him pay."

He leaned closer, his breath warm against her face, moonlight glittering off the barrel of the gun in his hand. "Don't worry, lady, you're going to get to see it. Well, at least some of it."

He turned suddenly, his pants brushing against her legs, and she studied his thin, hard face. It was pointed toward the road and she let her eyes follow his line of sight.

Headlights.

She could see them now.

See the headlights and hear the thrum of the motor. She was not a car person, but it sounded like Davis' vehicle. Besides, it wasn't likely anyone else would be out on such a back road this time of night.

Somehow, she had to warn Davis, but how? Yes, how, that was the question. But the trembling had started again and her brain was spinning. She bit her upper lip until she could taste blood, but no plan popped into her addled brain.

Maybe she could make a run for it. Shove the quiet woman down and run for the house. But that was crazy. Yes, she was having a good cancer day, but still she had no real strength. Plus, the man, what was his name? Oh yes, Lawton Turner. Vaguely, she recalled Davis speaking of him. Anyway, the man had a gun and he struck her as being someone who knew how to use it, and wasn't afraid to do so.

Speaking of guns, why hadn't they searched her? Was it because she was a woman? Or had they heard she'd been sick? She was conscious of the gun in her pocket; the weight was palpable. The man's face was still angled toward the road.

Ellen snuck a peek at the woman. Hard to be certain, but she appeared to be looking at the man. Ellen fingered the gun through her jeans. Sure, she knew how to shoot, but would she be quick enough when the time came? Would she have the nerve?

Out on the road, the SUV began to slow. Headlights swung down the drive. Damn, damn, damn, what was she going to do?

"Looks like it's show time," the man murmured. Then his free hand found Ellen's left arm and he was pulling her to him.

"All right now, lady, time for you to get ready to watch your husband face the music."

He leaned toward the quiet woman. "Ready, Tanya?"

"Yes," the woman whispered.

So, she could speak and she did have a name...Tanya. But why was the man telling her so much, giving her their names as if that didn't matter? Why? Why? Why?

When the answer came to her, she felt her knees start to buckle. She steadied herself as she considered the answer, an answer that scared her to the core.

"Okay then, you know what to do. Stay here and keep that gun on her until he gets out of the truck. Then march her forward into that light by the fence. Got that? It's so simple it will be easy. And all the time I'll have you covered."

"Okay, Lawton, I've got it."

"Once you get to the light, wait for me. I'll make the next move. Know what I mean?"

"Yes."

"Good. Now don't let me down, baby. This is important, Tanya, real important. We'll do what we talked about, then we'll be gone.

We're almost there, baby. No more than ten minutes and we'll be rolling. All right?

"Okay. I'm ready."

The woman sounded nervous, Ellen thought. Maybe she could talk to her, make some kind of a deal. Give them what they wanted. Money, or whatever. Maybe the woman would listen. She doubted the man would bargain, though. He didn't seem the type. But she had to try. She had to try soon. Give them what they wanted and they could be gone before Davis got out of his vehicle. Yes, she would try— it couldn't hurt to try.

Ellen turned, hoping to bargain with the man, but he was already gone, a shadow moving into deeper shadows. Shivering, she turned to speak to the woman, but there was a gun in her face. The woman held one finger across her own lips. The hand holding the gun was quite steady.

Sixty-eight

What room was that pistol in? Birdman knew he had seen the damn thing—had it been in a drawer? Not the kitchen and not the bathroom and he had been too scared to wander upstairs, so it had to be downstairs. In a bedroom, he figured. That was the most likely place. A bedroom or an office. His brain was always fuzzy and his memory unreliable, but he seemed to have seen it a room with a desk or a dresser, furniture like that. Birdman forced his trembling legs forward. God, but he needed a fix. His body still ached from Turner's beating and his mind was cloudy, like a mirror gone smoky.

He wandered from the kitchen into a room he thought of as an old-fashioned parlor, then walked into the dining room, then stepped into a room that rather defied description, but struck a chord. Sure, he remembered that old television and the bookcase full of paperbacks. His mind shifted, cleared, and he knew where to go. He moved quickly toward the round table where he seen the pistol next to a telephone.

Birdman could feel a smile curling his lips. A weapon would be just the thing; for sure he'd feel better knowing he had one. Maybe things would be all right after all. If he could only get through this night, he was heading out of state in the morning. He'd catch the first ride he could that was rolling west. Kansas had never sounded so good.

One look at the table and the trembling really took hold of him. The freaking pistol was missing. The table had a shallow drawer and Birdman jerked it open. All he could see were some rubber bands, an ink pen or two, a fistful of faded photographs of a young man he'd never seen, and a few loose keys that didn't do him one flipping bit of good.

Birdman looked hurriedly around the room, trying to choke down the panic that was rising in his mind like a flash flood. No gun on the TV, or the bookcase, or on either of the beds. Gone, the freaking gun was gone. What the hell was he going to do?

A woman's voice drifted into the room and he froze where he was, half in darkness, half in the faint light that filtered in from another room. Damn, probably the sheriff's wife talking. She sounded close and Birdman figured she was out on the porch. A portion of an old porch swing was visible through the window that faced the road. What the fuck was he going to do now? If she came back in the house right away, his ass was grass. But who was she talking to? Hell, it was the middle of the damn night. All the good people were supposed to be in bed. That left only the bad guys and Birdman wondered.

Then he heard a man speak and Birdman's his legs quivered, then slowly gave way. As he slunk to the floor, he started to pray. Not that prayer had ever helped him much, but what else did he have?

Birdman closed his eyes and listened. Listened harder than he had ever listened before.

At first, he could hear voices, mostly Lawton's, but then they died off and all he could hear was the porch swing creaking in the wind. Without warning, the wind died completely and he thought he could make out footsteps heading around the house.

When he opened his eyes, the first thing he saw was the gunrack on the wall. Birdman struggled to his feet. Maybe his luck was turning. He tiptoed across the floor and pulled the double-barreled shotgun from the rack. He was no hunter, but it was a heavy gun—at least it felt heavy to him—and he figured it would surely do considerable damage to a man. He'd shot one a few times with buddies, so he knew enough to thumb the safety off and pull the trigger.

As he turned to head for the back door, he wondered if the gun was loaded. He looked around for shells, but all he could see were old quilts stacked on a chair and more books lined up on the table, along with a couple of pictures hanging crooked on the wall. Only one thing left to do. Birdman prayed as he changed his grip on the shotgun.

Holding his breath, he flipped the lever and broke the gun open. Then he sucked in air as he mentally gave a short prayer of thanks. Both barrels were loaded. Birdman clicked the barrels closed, turned, and started for the back door, moving quickly, but watching where he placed his feet. Until he could get the hell away from Lawton Turner, silence was his best friend. After the loaded double-barrel, anyway.

He slipped out of the room, curled around the corner, then hustled through the kitchen and out on the back porch. Easing the door open, he cautiously stuck his head out, not wanting to do it, but recognizing he was better off knowing where Lawton Turner was.

All he could make out were shadowy objects, pools of moonlight, and the vast darkness he normally liked. Tonight, however, he didn't care one good hot damn for the darkness. The one man he feared most in the world was somewhere in that blackness and Birdman was afraid, bad afraid.

He swallowed as much of his fear as he could choke down, slipped out the door, and hurried into the night. Once he stepped off the concrete of the porch, he bent to his right, curled around behind the old root cellar and climbed the mound of earth that covered the cellar. Here, he at least held the high ground. He watched enough black and white war movies to know that was important. Of course, John Wayne he wasn't. And he wasn't counting heavy on the cavalry cresting the rise anytime soon.

Sixty-nine

The crunch of gravel beneath the tires of his SUV sounded good to Davis. The night felt long to him, elastic, stretched so much it felt as though it had reached the breaking point. Too much stress, he figured; that, and not enough sleep. Maybe he would sleep tonight. But as Tanya's face flashed across his brain, he knew it was going to be another long night.

He rolled on up the driveway, glad to be home, yet dreading the night that stretched before him. Gradually, he became aware of lights off to his left. What in the world?

His eyes shifted west. Crap, almost every light in the house was on. Ellen should have been in bed hours ago. Had something happened? Damn. What if Ellen had needed him? He never should have gone to the bar. Shit. Davis pressed down on the accelerator, spinning gravel, cursing himself for acting like such a jerk.

A moment later, he braked to a stop, shifted into park, and cut the motor as he popped the door. All those lights, all those lights. Maybe they meant nothing. Maybe Ellen was simply awake and wandering around. Maybe he should stay home more. Maybe, maybe, maybe. Suddenly he was full of maybes. He started toward the house, hurrying, eyes fixed on the lights, his mind flickering thoughts like images cast by an old movie projector.

He reached the fence and put his left hand on the gate, thinking what he would say to Ellen if she was up. As he pulled the gate open, he heard the voice.

"That'll be far enough, Mr. Sheriff."

Davis could feel his guts kinking up as he forced himself to turn slowly, not knowing for sure, but having a pretty damn good idea who the voice belonged to. Even so, a chill ran through his veins when Lawton Turner stepped into the light.

"Now ease that gun out of its holster and toss it on the ground. And do it real nice and slow, unless you want to die real quick."

Davis couldn't see where he had much choice. He didn't like it, but the business end of the automatic in Turner's hand was steady and he had no doubt Turner would pull the trigger if he needed, or wanted to. Police officers had an old saying about never giving up your weapon, but he didn't trust Lawton Turner to put much stock in that. Besides, he had no clue where Ellen was and he couldn't take any chances. Some nights, when sleep proved elusive, she took walks. No way he could allow her to walk into a firefight. None of his options was any good. Buying a few minutes seemed the best of them. He had to hope Turner would make a mistake, one that he could take advantage of. Getting shot immediately took that possibility out of play.

Moving slowly, he eased his nine-millimeter out of his holster, bent, and gently tossed it out in the yard, wondering what would happen next. Whatever it was, Davis didn't figure that it would be good.

~ * ~

"Smart move, Sheriff. You've bought yourself another five minutes. But before we get there, I've got a surprise for you." Lawton felt a grin snake crawling across his face. He was a man who had long prided himself on not revealing his emotions, but this was a moment he'd been waiting on for over two years and he aimed to enjoy it.

"Tanya?"

"Right here.

"Showtime. Bring her on out."

Lawton could hear footsteps, but he kept his eyes on the sheriff's face. Not for all the money in Pratt County would he have missed Davis Wells' expression when his wife stepped out of the shadows.

He heard the sheriff gasp, then watched as the man's face went from shock to fear to anger. Next, it changed to a look Lawton couldn't quite decipher, at least without some study, but he had no intention of letting the situation linger. Already, it was an hour later than he had figured on and he aimed to be deep in Kansas before daylight broke.

He couldn't risk even a quick glance at the women. Davis Wells was no easy mark. He'd have to trust Tanya this time. "You got her covered?"

"Yes."

"Any trouble?"

"None."

"See anybody else around?"

"Like who?"

"How the hell should I know? If I knew, I wouldn't have to ask you, now would I? Just answer the damn question."

"All right, all right. Don't get mad. I haven't seen anybody else. Lawton?"

"Yep."

"It's getting real late. Don't you think we need to get going?"

"Damn it, Tanya, I know how late it is, and, yeah, we need to rock and roll. So, Mrs. Wells, you need to step on out real good into that light and get ready to tell your husband goodbye. Hear you're sick and all, but you need to know before it's too late that he's been out whoring around on you, ain't that right, Sheriff?"

"No, Lawton, that isn't right. Now, you've had your fun. Let's call an end to this circus before somebody gets hurt."

"Too late for that, asshole. For more than two years you've made me pay. Now it's your turn to pay. And you're going to pay hard, you prick. You best get prepared."

~ * ~

Davis glanced at Ellen, trying to catch her eye. But this night his luck was lousy. He shifted his eyes to the man holding the gun.

"Before this gets any more out of hand, let me ask you something, Turner."

"Guess we can call that your last request, Sheriff. What do you want to know?"

Davis made his face hard. He had a truly bad feeling this night wasn't going to have any sort of a happy ending, but he didn't see what he could do except prolong the preliminaries and pray for a miracle, or two. Besides, there were a couple of things he wanted to know for sure before time ran out.

"I want to know if you're the one responsible for all the bad fentanyl. For all the ODs the last few weeks."

Lawton snickered. "You might say that."

"And you selected each victim because they had some connection to me."

"Give the man a kewpie doll."

Davis felt sick at his stomach. Part of him wanted to rush Turner, take a chance that he could get to him before he could pull the trigger. If he did that, he'd be a moving target. But another part of him, the realistic part of his brain, knew that was a bad gamble, one almost certainly destined to end in failure, and sudden death. No, talking was his best bet, at least until a better option came along.

"That's what we thought, me and my deputies. You know, Turner, that every single one of them is out tonight looking for you. Truth is, a couple of them are scheduled to stop by here any time and give me an update."

Davis doubted Turner would believe him, but he had to try something. Maybe Turner would believe something he said, give him a legitimate chance to pull the situation out of the fire. He thought about what Turner had said about him cheating. That would be an issue even if he took care of Turner. Davis supposed he could always pass off the man's comments about his fooling around as spite, as a lie.

If Turner didn't bite, maybe he could at least erode some of the man's confidence, put enough doubt in his mind to slow him down—even a fraction of a second might make a difference. Davis figured now was the only time he had to lay it on thick.

"Why not just call it a night, Turner? Now, I'm not fool enough to think you're simply going to lower your weapon and give yourself up. So why not just ease on out into the dark and make tracks. You and your woman. Ellen and I will give you our cell phones so we can't call for help, and if you leave before my deputies get here, you'll have a nice head start. Tonight doesn't have to end bad. Not for you and your woman. Not for me and mine. Just back on out of here and I promise I'll cut you a break."

Davis licked his lips and swallowed. His throat felt tight, dry. Damn, he needed a drink. But that wasn't in the cards, either. He had to keep talking. What choice did he have?

"Tell you what, Lawton, you tell me which way you're headed after you leave here and I'll tell my deputies you took off in the opposite direction. You tell me you guys are rolling west and I'll swear you headed east. You've got to admit that's fair. What do you say, Turner?"

"I say you can eat shit and die. Since I learned better at sixteen, I've never believed one goddamn word the law says, and you're the last asshole on earth I'd believe. No sir, there'll be no walking away from here. Anyway, not till I finish what I came to do. Which, you son-of-a-bitch, is shoot you right between the eyes."

Turner grinned. "Only first, you prick, you're going to watch your wife die."

Seventy

She turned her body as she stepped forward, trying not to be obvious, but angling so that the pistol in the jeans was further away from the man with the gun. Somehow, she had to find a way to get it out. Doing it without getting either Davis or herself shot was going to be the problem. She'd have to create a distraction, one that would grab the attention of both the man and the woman behind her. What name had the man called the woman? Tanya? Yes, that was it. Maybe someday she'd have a chance to testify against her. If she made it through this night, that is.

She glanced at Davis. For a moment, their eyes met and she thought he seemed be trying to send her a message. His lips moved as though he were forming silent words, but the light was too chancy to make them out. She shook her head an inch or two and gave him the best smile she could muster as she subtly patted the pocket of her jeans that held the gun.

Ellen shifted her gaze to the man with the gun in his hand. So he was the infamous Lawton Turner. Davis had spoken of him often enough for her to know she had to be extra careful. Lawton Turner worried her a lot more than the woman standing behind her. Ellen had gotten a good look at her in the circle of light cast by the security light, and right away she'd seen that the other woman was nervous. Had the wind up, her dad would have said. For a moment, Ellen wondered what he would have done if he were in her place. Then she shook her head and eased a half-step to her left, a few more inches away from the man she feared most in the world.

Her lips felt dry and she longed for a long cool drink of water. But that was only wishful thinking, and, despite what Davis had said, she wasn't expecting any deputies to roll down the drive any time soon. If they were going to get out of this mess, it was going to be up to her and Davis. The really bad thing was only one of them had a gun. For a second, she wondered about the man Davis had told her about, the informant. If he had any sense, he'd have hightailed it long ago. Moving as casually as she could, she let her right hand slip lower, and lower, and lower, slipping until she could feel the outline of the gun beneath the texture of her jeans.

Seventy-one

Davis caught the look in Ellen's eye and tried to smile for her. Somehow, he had to get them out of this fucking mess. Somehow, he had to make things right. Somehow, he would do it. Somehow.

He remembered then the lie he had told Turner about his deputies swinging by any minute to report and allowed his mind to fantasize for a few seconds about that happening. But he knew that was only a dream, and dreams rarely came true. Shifting his eyes, he stared over Ellen's left shoulder at the face of the woman he'd kissed not an hour before, trying to get his mind around the fact that the whole damn thing had been a setup. A fucking setup. She'd never really been interested in him.

Angled this way, he couldn't see Turner's face, but Tanya's looked nervous, her eyes darting and flickering, her face open and expectant. She would give him his cue. If he'd read Ellen right, she had a gun in one pocket of her jeans, so if he could get to it somehow, or give her a chance to use it, they still might get out of this mess.

Tanya was the weak link. No way this side of hell Lawton Turner was going to fold his cards. The man was way too tough an hombre for that. Davis figured his best bet was to count on the woman making a mistake. It wasn't much of a chance, but it was more than he'd thought he had a minute before.

Tanya's eyes shifted and he knew she was looking at Lawton. Hoping the bastard was looking back at her, Davis eased closer to Ellen, moving as smoothly and quietly as possible, more sliding his feet across the grass than stepping. Going slowly—a couple of inches at a time, but moving in the right direction.

He risked a glance at his wife, but she was looking at Turner, too. Fear crawled across her face and Davis knew time was running out. Taking a chance, he took a step in her direction, noticing as he did Ellen's right hand rubbing the right front pocket of the jeans. She'd lost so much weight with the cancer that the jeans hung loose on her. But he'd bet money that pocket was big enough to hold the old snub nose .38. That S&W was a good gun, one you could rely on. And Ellen knew how to use it—he'd taught her himself. Therefore, the question became would she use it if he could give her the chance?

Davis quickly studied his wife's face. Frightened, yes. But who wouldn't be in similar circumstances? He figured he looked a bit scared himself. Which was all right, because he was, and with good reason. Lawton Turner was a real badass, not some kid breaking windows, or a homeless man shoplifting, or even a druggie like Birdman.

His mind froze. Remembering Birdman made him wonder. Where the hell was that drughead? He was supposed to be in the old garage. Surely all the talking had aroused his interest. A man who lived in the shadows like Birdman had to be constantly worrying about the law, or whether some dealer he owed was coming in on his blind side, or if some drunk punks were out scouting around for some down-and-out like him to pulverize. Unless he was high, he was bound to have taken notice of the commotion. So where was he? Had he already cut-and-run, or was he out there in the dark, hunkered down, scared shitless?

Then Turner spoke and there wasn't any time left to worry about Birdman, his deputies, or the man-in-the-moon. He had to make his play and do it now. Win, lose, or draw, he'd come to the end of the line. Words didn't matter any longer. Action was the only thing that counted. Davis knew he had to get it right the first time. Lawton Turner was not a man to grant any second chances.

Seventy-two

"Alrighty now, it's showtime." Lawton Turner took a step forward. "Any last requests, Sheriff? Aw, too bad. I was so hoping to hear you beg a little. Perhaps we'll get there yet."

Turner jerked his head at Tanya. "All right, baby, have Mrs. Davis take two steps forward. Then shoot her in the back of the head. Watching his wife's brains getting blown out of her skull should work just fine as the last sight the bastard ever sees."

Tanya shivered. How had it really come to this? All along she'd thought Lawton would back out at the last minute. Surely he'd already scared the sheriff and his wife enough—taught them a damn fine lesson, as he would say.

She risked a glance at Lawton. He glared back at her and she looked away, forcing her eyes on the woman standing no more than three or four yards in front of her. She had nothing in the world against this woman. Actually, the woman should have been the one to have something against her. She'd been actively seducing her husband. Damn, what a freaking mess she'd gotten herself into this time.

It wasn't something she'd planned do, but Tanya found herself shifting her eyes to Davis. He was staring at her, she could see that, but he was too far away for her to read the expression on his face. He appeared tense, as though he were nerving up, going to do something, and do it soon. No matter what she had done, she'd always thought of him as a tough man, a man not to cross. She'd warned Lawton.

"Tanya, it's time."

She heard Lawton's voice; she understood the words; she certainly knew what they meant. But her head was spinning and she felt slightly dizzy. The gun felt heavy in her hand. Tanya felt sure it was shaking. How the hell would she ever pull the trigger?

"Tanya. Now."

Her insides were quivering. She told herself she could do this. That she could do it for Lawton. But...

"Now, Tanya."

"Lawton..."

"I said now. Do it, do it now."

Tanya closed her eyes as her finger tightened on the trigger.